VINEYARD
SHADOWS

Also by Philip R. Craig
in Large Print:

Vineyard Blues
A Fatal Vineyard Season
A Shoot on Martha's Vineyard
A Deadly Vineyard Holiday

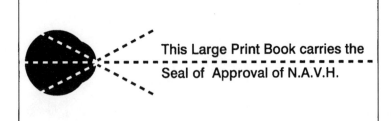

VINEYARD SHADOWS

A MARTHA'S VINEYARD MYSTERY

PHILIP R. CRAIG

Thorndike Press • Waterville, Maine

Published in 2001 by arrangement with Scribner, an imprint of Simon & Schuster, Inc.

Thorndike Press Large Print Mystery Series.

The tree indicium is a trademark of Thorndike Press.

The text of this Large Print edition is unabridged.
Other aspects of the book may vary from the original edition.

Set in 16 pt. Plantin by Myrna S. Raven.

Printed in the United States on permanent paper.

Library of Congress Cataloging-in-Publication Data

Craig, Philip R., 1933–
    Vineyard shadows: a Martha's Vineyard mystery /
Philip R. Craig.
      p. cm.
    ISBN 0-7862-3646-9 (lg. print : hc : alk. paper)
    1. Jackson, Jeff (Fictitious character) — Fiction.
2. Private investigators — Massachusetts — Martha's
Vineyard — Fiction. 3. Martha's Vineyard (Mass.) —
Fiction. 4. Large type books. I. Title.
PS3553.R23 V53 2001b
  813′.54—dc21   2001048019

For our grandson, Riley Spenser Craig,
a fifth-generation Vineyarder,
and for his other grandparents,
Bob and Buzzy Gardner

"What are you thinking of?
    What thinking? What?
"I never know what you are thinking.
    Think."
I think we are in rats' alley
Where the dead men lost their bones.
                    — T. S. Eliot
                    The Waste Land

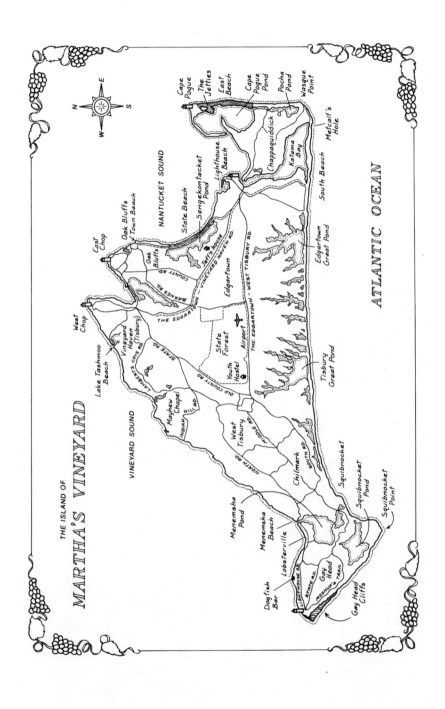

THE ISLAND OF
MARTHA'S VINEYARD

1

I got the details by talking with the survivors, since I wasn't at the house when it happened. Instead, I was on the clam-flats in Katama with my son Joshua. When we came home, there was a cop at the head of our driveway and an ambulance was pulling out and heading toward the hospital in Oak Bluffs. I turned into something made of ice.

The cop recognized my old Land Cruiser and waved us in. I drove fast down our long, sandy driveway. The yard was full of police cars and uniforms. Sergeant Tony D'Agostine met me as I stepped out of the truck.

I was full of fear. "Stay here," I said to Joshua, and shut the truck's door behind me.

"There's been some trouble," said Tony.

"Where's Zee? Where's Diana?!"

"Take it easy," said Tony, "it's all over."

"Where are they?!" I pushed him aside, and went toward the house. He followed me, saying something I wasn't hearing. I saw what looked like blood on the grass. Jesus! Cops stood aside as I came through them.

That was the beginning of it for me.

The day had started earlier, of course, and had seemed like any other day. School was out, so the pale June people were already on the island, trying to brown up on the beaches before going back to their mainland jobs. Parking places were getting hard to find on the main streets of the Vineyard's towns, and the harbors were beginning to fill with boats. Another summer season was under way.

That morning, after breakfast, Zee had had a date with Manny Fonseca down at the Rod and Gun Club, where she would practice her pistol shooting under his sharp eye in preparation for an upcoming competition.

"I'm taking Diana," Zee had said. "She's been on my case for weeks. She wants to watch, and I guess this is as good a time as any."

Competitive pistol shooting was an odd recreation for Nurse Zee, because she was a healer who basically disapproved of firearms; but, as she had discovered to her surprise and sometimes consternation, she was what Manny called a "natural" with a pistol. Worse yet, she had found that she enjoyed competitive shooting. These facts notwithstanding, she scorned Manny's NRA clichés about the benefits of gun possession and was ever ill at ease about having a couple firearms of her own, including the custom .45 that she used in competition.

"Just remember what Shane told Marian," I told her when she got into one of her antifirearms moods. " 'A gun is just a tool. It's as good or bad as the person using it.' "

"It may be a tool for Shane," said Zee, "but for me it's a toy. That makes it even more stupid and immoral."

"Target shooting isn't stupid or immoral," I said. "It gives you pleasure. Pleasure is good. Ask any hedonist."

"Guns are dangerous. We'd be better off if no one had any!"

There were times when I thought that myself, of course. But although I almost never used them, I still kept my father's 30.06 and shotguns in the gun cabinet, along with the old .38 I'd carried when I was a Boston cop.

"Maybe," I said, "but people do have them. I have them. You have them. They're not going to go away. It's better to know how to use them safely and to enjoy them than to wish there weren't any."

"I know. But I don't always like it."

That morning I'd just said, "Well, make sure the girl child has her earplugs and glasses. I don't need a deaf daughter."

11

"What's deaf mean, Pa?" Diana the Huntress, who spent a great deal of time looking for food, had asked.

"It means you can't hear. Like when you put your fingers in your ears. Shooting is very noisy, and the noise can hurt your ears, so you always wear earplugs when you shoot. And you wear shooting glasses in case something hits you in the eye."

"Oh." Diana had put her fingers in her ears, and smiled up at me. Then she had pointed and said, "Can I have that piece of toast you didn't eat?"

"Sure."

I had gone to the tide chart that was taped to the refrigerator. "Well, since you ladies are going shooting, I guess I will go clamming. If I leave right now, the tide will be just right down-harbor." I had looked at my growing son. "You want to come, Josh?"

"Yes, Pa."

Joshua liked to do what his folks did. Such a manly little chap. Just like his dad.

So he and I had collected our gloves and clam baskets and driven to Katama, full of innocence, not knowing how our lives were about to be changed.

Back at home, Zee packed her shooting gear into the flight bag she used to tote her stuff, washed and stacked the breakfast dishes, and, just before ten, headed out the door with Diana.

As she reached her little Jeep, she heard a car coming down the driveway. She put the flight bag on the hood of the Jeep and turned, thinking it was me, coming back early for some reason.

But it wasn't me. It was a black car with tinted windows. Zee didn't recognize it. The car stopped and for a while nothing else happened. Then doors opened and two men got out. They wore slacks and loose summer shirts that hung down over their belts. Dark glasses covered their eyes. One was a normal-sized man. The other one was the size of a large refrigerator.

Zee stepped forward to meet them. Diana came, too, and took Zee's hand.

"Can I help you, gentlemen?"

"I'll bet you can," said the refrigerator. A little wind caught his shirttail and lifted it slightly, giving Zee a brief glimpse of a pistol holstered on his belt. His black glasses seemed to eat her up.

"We want to see Tom Rimini," said the other man.

"I'm afraid you've come to the wrong house," said Zee. "I don't know any Tom Rimini."

"You Mrs. Jackson?"

She nodded, feeling uneasy.

"Then we're at the right house. We don't want no trouble, so you better just have him step out." Somehow both of them had gotten very close to her.

She pulled Diana nearer to her. "I just told you. I don't know anyone named Tom Rimini."

"That's not what we hear," said the refrigerator. He put out a huge hand and took hold of the collar of her shirt. "Don't get yourself hurt for him. It won't do no good."

She jerked herself away from him and felt the shirt tear. She was both angry and frightened. "I don't know who you are, but you'd better get back in that car and get out of here right now!"

"Oh, a feisty one," said the refrigerator. "I like feisty ones, Howie. Nice tits, too." He laughed.

"This your little girl?" asked Howie. "Come here, dearie."

He swept Diana up into his arms before Zee knew what he was doing.

"Ma! Ma!" cried Diana.

Zee reached for her, but the refrigerator stepped between her and Howie.

"Ma! Ma!" he said, grinning and spreading his arms. Zee ducked, but he was

14

expecting her move and caught her. "Hold it, Ma."

But Zee didn't hold it. She stamped her foot on his shin and brought her knee up hard. It was as though he could read her mind. He turned slightly and the knee glanced off his thigh. Then he slapped her across the face and her ears rang. He slapped her again and she felt sickness rise up in her. She twisted in his arms and this time he let her go. She almost fell.

"Give me my daughter!"

"Take it easy," said Howie. "And you take it easy, too, Pat. We don't want any trouble, Mrs. Jackson. We just want Tom Rimini. We get him, we go away. Just like that."

She felt so light-headed that she could hardly stand. "I tell you he isn't here. I've never heard of him."

"Go look in the house, Pat," said Howie.

"Keep an eye on Ma," said Pat. "She may jump you when I'm gone."

"I don't think so," said Howie. He held Diana against his chest with his left hand and dipped his right hand under his shirt. The hand came out, and there was a click, and the hand was holding a knife with a long, thin blade. He laid it on Diana's cheek. "You won't jump me, will you, Mrs. Jackson?"

She stepped back. "No. Please take the knife away. I'll do whatever you want, but don't hurt her."

"That's good," said Howie. "Pat, go search the house."

"She don't act so tough now," said Pat. He went into the house.

"I hope Rimini ain't in there," said Howie. "If he is, Pat is going to be pretty pissed off at you."

"He's not! You've come to the wrong house, I tell you. Please, let Diana go. Let her come to me. We won't run or fight. We'll do what you want."

"You'll do what we want, anyway," said Howie.

Pat came out of the house. "Nobody home." He looked at Zee. "When'll the rat be back?"

"How many times do I have to tell you that he's not here? I never heard of him. You must have gotten bad information."

Pat came toward her with long strides. She backed away, but he caught her arm with a huge hand. "They had a talk with his wife like I'm talking with you," said Pat. "Like this." He hit her in the belly and she fell, doubled over, unable to breathe, feeling her mouth sucking air like a fish out of water. She didn't hurt; she just couldn't move.

"You don't think she'd lie, do you?" asked Pat.

"You're a pretty woman," said Howie conversationally. "Pat's got an eye for a pretty woman. Now you stop lying and maybe I can talk him into looking for Rimini someplace else."

She tried to speak, but could not. They watched her with detachment. Finally she could breathe. There was grass and dirt in her mouth. She was filled with fear for Diana.

"I'm not lying, I swear. If I knew him, I'd tell you."

Pat picked her up and tore her shirt half off her body. "Oh, I don't know," he said. "You're a tough chicken. You probably need more persuading than most."

He hit her and knocked her backward against the Jeep. She struck the flight bag with one flailing arm and knocked it to the ground. She tried to stand, but the world turned gray, then black, and she fell.

Far away she heard Diana cry, "Ma! Ma! Don't hit my ma! Don't hit my ma!"

"Don't hit her too hard, Pat," said Howie's voice. "She can't talk if she's dead, and sometimes you don't know your own strength."

The world swam back out of blackness.

17

The flight bag was underneath her.

"You and me are going to have some fun first," Pat said to her. "Then if you be polite and tell us what we want to know, you can stay pretty for your husband. Get up now."

She nodded and, using her body to shield her hands, slid them into the bag. "All right," she said. "Please don't hit me again. I'll get up." She touched the familiar grip of the .45. "I'm dizzy. I just need a minute." She got the pistol in one hand and a full clip in the other. She knew she had to be very fast and very sure, because she'd only get one chance.

"All right," she said. "I'm getting up now."

She straightened up on her knees and turned the gun toward Pat, slapping the clip into the magazine as she did.

Pat, caught off guard, was still almost too quick. As she jacked a round into the firing chamber, he leaped back and with remarkable speed whipped a hand to his belt and came up with his own pistol.

She shot him three times, one, two, three. The first round took him in the belly and knocked him back as his own weapon went off. She was aware of a blow to her left ribs but paid it no heed as her second round hit him in the chest and sent his pistol flying.

Her third round split his dark glasses in two and left him spread-eagled on the lawn like some profane crucified Christ.

She was on her feet before he hit the ground and was walking toward huge-eyed Howie, her pistol now held in both hands.

"Let go of my daughter!"

But Howie had seen what had happened to Pat. He clutched Diana to his chest and put the knife to her throat as he backed toward the black car.

"You try to shoot me, and the kid gets it! I ain't kidding! You put down that gun, or else!"

He touched the knife tip to Diana's throat and a trickle of blood ran down from the wound.

Zee shot him in the right elbow and his knife arced away. He screamed and she shot him in the knee, below Diana's thrashing legs. He screamed again and went down. Diana, agile as a monkey, rolled away and ran to her mother.

"Ma! Ma!"

Zee knelt and tipped up her daughter's chin. The knife wound was shallow, superficial.

"Go inside and get the telephone and the first aid kit and bring them out to me."

"Yes, Ma. Ma, I'm scared."

19

Her mother put a smile on her face, and gave her a hug. "Everything is all right, now. No need to be scared anymore. Now, go bring me those things."

"Yes, Ma."

Diana went into the house and Zee walked over to sobbing Howie and put the muzzle of the .45 under his chin.

"Don't kill me!" cried Howie. "Please don't kill me! Get me a doctor!"

She took a pistol from his belt and another from an ankle, then stood up and went to Pat's body. He lay on his back with his arms outstretched and his fly unzipped. He had no backup pistol, probably because he was so big he hadn't thought he needed more than one. She collected his pistol from where it had fallen on the lawn and went to meet Diana.

She dialed 911, reported shots fired and at least one man dead, then sat down on the porch steps and cleaned and dressed the cut in Diana's throat.

"You're hurt, too, Ma," said Diana, pointing.

There was blood on the left side of what remained of Zee's shirt and, seeing it, Zee was aware of a pain in her side. Lifting the shirt away from her body, she saw the furrow of Pat's bullet over her ribs. She pushed and probed her ribs enough to be fairly certain that none were broken, then cleaned and dressed that wound, too.

Across the yard, Howie was moaning and crying. She watched him, feeling nothing for a while, but then crossed over to him as the first of the sirens came down her driveway, and began to care for him.

"This was all for nothing," she told him. "I never heard of Tom Rimini."

"Jesus," groaned Howie, and fainted.

A half an hour later I came home.

2

Zee and Diana were sitting in lawn chairs, surrounded by medics and cops. I felt my life come back to me. I ran to them and took them in my arms.

"My God, what happened? Are you all right?"

Zee winced, but smiled. There was an odd look in her eyes. "Easy on the rib cage, Jeff! Yes, we're both fine. I'm so glad you're here."

"Me, too, Pa," said Diana, hanging on to my neck.

"Me, too," said a medic. "Your wife and your daughter should both be up at the hospital, to make sure they're as good as they think they are. But Zee here wouldn't go until you came home. Now you're home, so tell both of them to get into the ambulance!"

He sounded testy.

I loosened my hold on Zee. "What's wrong? You're not all right." I saw now that her lip was split and her face was bruised. I touched her cheek and felt a cold fury grow inside me, driving away my fear and gratitude. "Who did this?"

"I'm just a little tender," said Zee, taking hold of my hands and kissing them. "This medic is right, though; Diana and I should go up to the hospital and have somebody look us over. It's just a precaution. We're really okay."

"Which is more than I can say for the other guys," said Tony D'Agostine, with a note of satisfaction in his voice.

"I'll go with you in the ambulance," I said to Zee.

"Not a good idea," said the medic. "The docs don't need you cluttering up the examining room. You can drive up in your own car."

"He's right," said Zee, and I knew he was, so I shut my mouth and let them take her and Diana away.

I looked around then and saw that Dom Agganis and Olive Otero of the State Police were there, along with Edgartown's cops and Manny Fonseca. I was the only one who didn't know what had happened.

Dom Agganis and Tony D'Agostine told me.

I didn't know what to say or think.

Manny Fonseca stepped closer. "I heard the shots from the club, and when Zee didn't show up for her lesson, I got worried and came here. Jesus, J.W., I couldn't believe my eyes. One guy dead, and the other all shot up. Couple of Boston hoods and she got 'em both. Five shots, five hits. Christ almighty!"

I began to come back to earth. "Who were they?" I asked Dom Agganis. "What were they doing here?"

"A couple of enforcers from Charlestown," said Agganis. "The dead one was Pat Logan. They call him — called him, I guess you'd better make that — 'The Pilot.' Pat 'The Pilot' Logan. Not because he was a pilot, you understand, but because he had the same name as the airport up in Boston. The other guy is Howie Trucker. I just ran a check on them. They both started young, then got into the business of robbing armored cars. It's traditional employment for the hoods in Charlestown, as you may know. Every up-and-coming wanna-be mobster does it or wants to. On the side, these two were muscle for hire. You ever hear of either of them?"

"No."

"I thought maybe you had dealings with them when you were on the Boston PD."

I thought back, then shook my head. "No. I've never known anybody from Charlestown."

"Just thought I'd ask. Anyway, they told your wife they were looking for a guy. I'm guessing that the guy crossed somebody and they were supposed to find him. Pat and Howie thought he was here at your house. He wasn't. They made a mistake."

"A big one for them," said Tony. He looked at Manny. "Jesus, Manny, you sure as hell taught Zee how to shoot!"

Manny said nothing.

"If they'd just taken her word for it that the guy wasn't here, none of this would have happened," said Olive Otero. "But they had to get tough." She shrugged. "Too bad for them."

Olive didn't look like she was about to shed any tears for Pat "The Pilot" or Howie Trucker.

My eyes found Zee's flight bag, which was back on the hood of her Jeep. Olive Otero noticed my look.

"We've taken your wife's pistol, since there's been a homicide. She may get it back later."

I nodded. It was standard procedure. "Sure. But why would two Charlestown hoods come here to our house? What made them think the guy was here?"

The cops exchanged glances. "Zee said she asked them that," said Tony. "They told her the guy's wife had told them he was here." Tony cocked his head to one side.

It made no sense to me. "The guy's wife? Like I told you, I don't know anybody in Charlestown. How could anybody in Charlestown even know where we live?"

"Maybe the guy and his wife don't live in Charlestown," said Agganis sensibly.

I obviously wasn't thinking very well. Being stupid wasn't going to help me a bit. I took a breath and pulled myself together. "What's the guy's name? Who were they looking for?"

"They were after a fella named Tom Rimini," said Agganis, studying me as he spoke. "Ever heard of him?"

Time stopped, then started again.

"What's the matter, J.W.? You okay?" Tony D'Agostine's voice sounded far away.

"Tom Rimini?" asked my voice.

"Yeah," said Dom Agganis. "You know the guy?"

I shook my head, more confused than before. "I never met him but I know of a man with that name. But I don't see how it could be him."

"If he's one of the slimeballs, I never heard of him," said Olive Otero. "But then I never heard of most of the scum in this state."

26

Officer Olive Otero was not my favorite cop. We had never hit it off. But I couldn't argue with her this time.

"The guy I'm thinking of isn't in the mob," I said. "He's a schoolteacher in Boston." I looked down into Olive's eyes. "My ex-wife married him after she left me."

Olive let that sink in. She had hard eyes. She said: "Left you, did she? And took up with this other guy?"

"You know how it is," I said. "I was a cop and she got tired of being scared all the time, wondering every night if I was going to come home, so she married a guy who didn't have to carry a pistol to work: another teacher she met at school. Tom Rimini. I think he teaches social studies."

Carla had been unhappy even before I'd gotten shot, but the shot was the last straw; she'd seen me through most of my rehab, but as soon as she was sure that I was going to be okay, she had told me she was divorcing me. I didn't argue. She told me she'd met a sweet man named Tom Rimini. She hoped I'd find a woman who could love me. I wished her well. When I got out of the hospital, I took a disability pension, sold the house in Somerville, and moved to the Vineyard. It took a while for me to get over Carla, because I don't love

27

easily or stop loving easily.

And now, years later, Tom Rimini had returned to my life.

"Why do you suppose somebody would send a couple of hoods after a schoolteacher?" asked Olive.

"I don't know."

"And why would his wife tell them he was here?" she went on. "She still mad at you after all this time, Mr. Jackson?"

I shook my head.

"Zee said they talked to Rimini's wife just like they were talking to Zee," Dom Agganis reminded her. "That means they slapped her around some, maybe beat her up good, maybe threatened her kids. Most people would tell them what they wanted to know."

"Well, where's Rimini, then? He's sure not here." Olive looked at me. "You sure you don't know nothing about this? If you do, you'd be smart to speak up now. Whoever sent these two down here may decide to send somebody else to do the job right. Somebody with more brains."

My temper rose, but I pushed it down. "I haven't seen my ex-wife in years, and I never met Rimini. But if some gang boss is after him, it's probably because Rimini owes him money or is under his skin in some other way. Howie Trucker probably knows. I think

28

we should have a talk with him."

"Not we," said Olive. "Not you, for sure. Just the cops. We don't need any civilians underfoot."

Anger moved my tongue. "You couldn't get information out of an encyclopedia, Olive!"

She shoved her face up toward mine. "You interfere with this criminal investigation and I'll have your ass in jail so fast it'll make your head spin!"

Dom Agganis stepped between us. "Now take it easy. Both of you back off. Starting with you, Officer Otero." She glared at him, hesitated, then stepped away. "You, too, J.W.," said Agganis. "We're all on the same side, here, remember."

I turned away. As I did, I heard Joshua's voice: "Pa! Pa! Can I get out now?"

Good grief, I'd forgotten all about him! I went to the Land Cruiser and opened the door.

"You forgot the clams, Pa. We need to put them in some salt water so they can spit out their sand."

"You're right," I said. More evidence that when violence and tragedy occur, the world keeps right on turning as if nothing unusual had happened. Probably, it hadn't.

"Where'd they take Ma and Diana?"

"She and your sister are up at the hospital. We'll go up and get them after we take care of the clams."

I went back to where Dom, Tony, and the others were still talking, and told them my plans.

"We're about done here," said Dom. "I'll have a wrecker come down and get the guys' car. If you think of anything that can help us, let me know."

"About this Rimini guy, for instance," said Olive.

I gave her a sour look and turned back to the truck.

Joshua and I got a pail of salt water down at the Sengekontacket landing, took it back to the house, and dumped our bucket of clams into it. Manny Fonseca was already gone, and most of the cops were drifting away.

"We'll be talking with your wife again later," said Agganis. "Get an official statement from her, maybe get some details she forgot."

"That new D.A. going to charge her with something?"

He shrugged. "Who knows. I doubt it, though. From what I've heard and seen here, I'd say it's a pretty open-and-shut case of self-defense. I know one thing: any lawyer would love to defend her — beautiful housewife attacked by professional thugs and leaving them spread on the lawn. That's movie stuff!"

Joshua and I got back into the old Toyota and drove to the hospital in Oak Bluffs. Zee worked in the emergency room, so when we came through the doors we were met by her colleagues and friends, including a doctor who looked like he belonged in high school.

"She's just fine," said a nurse. "They're both fine. That cut on your little girl's neck is just a scratch, really. Didn't even need stitches. And Zee's mostly got bruises. She'll be sore for a few days, but then she'll be good as new."

"She got shot. What about that?"

"She was very lucky. It just dug a sort of groove along her ribs. A couple of inches to the right and it would have been a different story, but that didn't happen. You want to see her?"

"Yes. Isn't she right here?"

The boy doctor came over and put out a small hand. "I'm Dr. Stone. Your wife is down the hall. I want to keep an eye on her until tomorrow. Just a precaution in case she experiences delayed shock. She also took a pretty good hit to the stomach, and I'd like to monitor the results of that for a while.

31

Your daughter can go home with you, though. Come on. I'll take you to them."

We followed him down the hall, and he led me to a room. Inside, Zee was propped up on the bed, reading Dr. Seuss to Diana, who was sitting beside her, looking at the pictures and making sure her mother got every word just right. Zee looked battered but beautiful. Her long, black hair was an ebony halo on the pillow.

"Hi," I said.

"Mom's reading *The Cat*," said Diana with a big smile.

Zee smiled, too. "I guess I'm here for the duration," she said.

"Just until tomorrow. It's just a precaution."

"I'd rather go home with you, but it's okay. Did the police tell you what happened?"

"Yes. I'm sorry I wasn't there. I'm sorry it happened. But you did the right thing."

She gave Diana a little push. "Get down, sweetie."

Diana and *The Cat* got off the bed and Zee put out her arms. I went over and got into them and she finally let herself cry and cry, cleaning the windows of her soul.

3

"I don't know if I'll ever get over this," said Zee when she finished her cry and was wiping her nose and eyes with a tissue.

"You will," I said. "It's a hell of a thing to have to kill somebody, but you didn't have any choice."

"Maybe I did have a choice. I keep thinking that maybe I did and just didn't take it." Her eyes were dark hollows in her battered face.

I felt anger. "Don't even think it! When men come after women with fists and guns, they deserve to be shot. You're not guilty of anything. You protected yourself and you protected Diana. That's what you're supposed to do, and you did it. I'm just glad that you were lucky enough to have the pistol handy and that you know how to use it. I owe Manny Fonseca more than I'll ever be able to pay him."

She shook her head. "Killing is bad. It's always bad."

"It may always be bad, but some killings are worse than others. It would have been worse if you'd let them kill you and Diana.

You made a good kill!"

"What a terrible phrase: 'a good kill.' That makes me a good killer."

I was making things worse. "Look," I said. "You're not a killer; you're a woman who shot two gunmen who had already beaten you, put a knife to our daughter's throat, and were about to do more of the same or worse. If another woman had done what you did, you'd be telling her what I'm telling you. You'd be right, and I'm right."

"I don't feel right."

I could understand that well enough. "You won't for a while," I said. "It took me a long time to get over killing that woman in Boston, but I finally did. It'll happen to you, too."

"Maybe."

"No maybe about it."

"But you were a cop and she was a thief and you didn't know it was a woman and you didn't shoot her until she shot you. I knew who I was shooting and I shot first."

"And a damned good thing, too. Pat Logan nearly got one into you anyway. When I cornered that woman in the alley that night, I'd have shot first if I'd known what she was going to do. You knew what those two guys were going to do."

"I thought I knew. Maybe I was wrong."

34

"Tell me," I said, angry at her for having such thoughts, "do you really think you were wrong? Now, here, do you think you were wrong? I sure as hell don't."

She held my hand for what seemed a long time, then squeezed it. "I don't know, but I know I don't like it."

"There's nothing to like about it," I said, "but you did the right thing. Know that." I kissed her. "I love you. And I thank you for saving yourself and Diana."

She put her arms around me.

"Ma," said Diana, who had been very patient. "We never finished *The Cat*."

Zee wiped her eyes again and smiled at her kid. "No, we didn't. Let's do that before you go home with your dad."

"I'll come up," said Diana, and did that.

"Me, too," said Joshua, who wasn't too old for another reading of *The Cat*. He climbed up the other side of the bed. It was a close fit for three, but they managed it.

"While you're finishing the story," I said, "I'm going to tend to some other business. I'll be back."

"Where are you going?" asked Zee.

"Out. What will I do? Nothing."

Before she could say more, I left. I went back to the emergency room and found a nurse. There was a clipboard on the desk beside her. It had a ballpoint pen hooked to the board with a string.

"I need to talk with the officer who's watching over Howard Trucker," I said. "The man they brought in with gunshot wounds."

"Oh," she said. "Well, you can't talk with Mr. Trucker, if that's what you have in mind."

"No, I just need to speak with the officer."

"Well, I guess that's all right." She told me where they had Howie. "They're going to fly Mr. Trucker up to Boston as soon as the helicopter gets here," she added. "He may lose an arm."

"A one-armed strong-arm man, eh?"

"That's not funny, J.W.! I heard what he did to Zee, but he's still a human being, after all!"

"Maybe."

She turned away and I snagged the clipboard and walked back down the hall.

The room wasn't too far down the hall from Zee. There was a young Oak Bluffs cop seated on a chair beside the door. I didn't know him, which was good. With my clipboard in my hand, I walked up to him. I was in civvies, but that didn't make any difference in the M.V. hospital because half the doctors came to work in jeans and sandals. I looked at the clipboard and tried to form my face into that expressionless mask that physicians apparently learn in doctor school.

"The helicopter is on its way," I said, barely glancing at the cop. "I'll be in here a few minutes. If I'm still here when they land, let me know." I offered him a thoughtful frown and went by him into the room. The young cop never said a word. I shut the door behind me.

I'd half-expected to find a nurse or someone else in the room, but Howie was alone. He was not in good shape. He had tubes feeding into him and some sort of cast or wrapping on his right arm and his leg. There were wires leading from him to monitoring devices of various kinds. His eyes were dull and his breathing was shallow. I figured they probably had him on painkillers, at least. I didn't think I had much time.

I went to the bed and slapped his face. His bleary eyes came into focus. I leaned down.

"Can you hear me, Howie?"

A pause, then a nod. "Yeah."

"There's a helicopter coming to take you to a bigger hospital in Boston."

"Yeah. Good."

"But you won't be on it, Howie, unless you talk to me."

"Wha . . . whatta you mean?"

I leaned closer. "I'm Jackson. I'm the husband."

Sudden fear widened his eyes.

I held the ballpoint pen in front of those wide eyes. "You know what this is, Howie?"

"Yeah. It's a pen. Whatta you want, for God's sake?"

"I want to know who hired you to do this job. You tell me, and I walk out that door, and you fly up to Boston. You don't tell me, I'm going to jam this pen up your nose and into your brain. Now, who hired you?"

Howie opened his mouth too wide. He had yelling instead of talking in mind. I covered his mouth with my hand and his eyes bulged.

With my other hand, I put the point of the pen up his left nostril. "If you don't tell me, I'll find out some other way," I said. I wiggled the pen and his nose began to bleed. "This is your last chance." I took my hand away from his mouth and he gasped weakly for breath.

"Sonny Whelen," he said. "Sonny sent us. Don't kill me."

"Why is he after Tom Rimini?"

"I don't know. He never said."

I wiggled the pen some more, and Howie's voice rose. "I swear it. He never said why! He just wanted Rimini!"

"Why did you come to my house?"

I didn't think Howie's eyes could get any bigger. "The woman, Rimini's wife, she told 'em! She said Rimini was here. She gave 'em the address. They roughed her up and she talked. Jesus, take that pen away. Don't kill me! Please!"

I took the pen out of his nose. "If you're lying to me, I'll find you again," I said.

"I'm telling you the truth," moaned Howie. "I swear to God!"

I wondered what Howie's God thought of that oath. Not much more than I did, I guessed. I patted Howie's cheek, straightened and walked out, shutting the door behind me.

"How's he doing?" asked the young cop.

"As well as can be expected. The helicopter should be here soon." I walked away.

Around a corner in the hall I leaned the clipboard against a wall where someone would find it, and went on to Zee's room, arriving just as she was closing the book that told the tale of *The Cat in the Hat*.

"Perfect timing." Zee smiled a beautiful battered smile.

"We should leave you alone so you can get some rest," I said.

"I'm fine," said Zee.

"We'll give the docs twenty-four hours to make sure you're right about that," I said. "We'll be back in the morning."

"Bring me some clean clothes."

"Only if you promise to take them off later."

"Deal."

I kissed her, collected the kids, and went home. On the way, Diana gave us her version of what had happened:

The bad men had come and one of them had grabbed her and scared her and hurt her with a knife. It wasn't really a bad hurt, though, because it didn't even take a stitch. But one of the bad men had hurt Ma a lot, and Diana was more scared than ever. The bad man hit Ma, and knocked her down. Diana had kicked and tried to get away, but the bad man with the knife was too strong. Then Ma got her pistol and shot the bad men and Diana got away and Ma had put a Band-Aid on her boo-boo, and the police came and then the ambulance had taken them to the hospital with the siren blowing.

"I hope you're not scared anymore," I said. "It's all over. The bad guys lost and they won't be back."

"I know," said Diana. "One of them is dead and the other one is almost dead, and Ma and I are good." She nodded her little head. Things had worked out as they were supposed to. I remembered Chesterton's observation that children, being innocent, prefer justice, while, adults, being sinful, prefer mercy.

I felt a tug on my elbow. It was Joshua. "Pa," he said. "I'm hungry."

I looked at my wristwatch. Holy smoke! It was noon. A lot had happened that morning.

"What do you say we go down to the Dock Street Coffee Shop for lunch?" I asked. "You can have whatever you want."

"Yes! Yes!"

"Can we have ice cream afterward?"

"Sure."

So we drove down into Edgartown and found a parking place on Summer Street. The dreaded summer meter maids were not hard at work yet, so we stood a good chance of not getting a ticket. We walked over to Main Street, took a left toward the harbor, and another left on Dock Street. At the far end of the Coffee Shop counter there were three stools in a row, and we took them. The waitress came and we ordered and then watched the cook at work. He was a thing of beauty, never wasting a motion. The food came and it was good. Afterward, up on North Water Street, we got ice cream. It was

41

a lovely June day, and the streets and shops were full of tourists who knew nothing of the bloody business that had taken place at my house only hours before.

"That was good, Pa." The kids licked their fingers.

We went back up Main Street. At the corner of Summer and Main, the Chief of the Edgartown Police was teaching a young summer cop how to direct traffic. I waved and the Chief gave me a sour look as he lifted a hand in reply. His student was not a fast learner, apparently.

At home, the children played in the yard while I worked to wash away the last signs of the blood on the grass. When it was as gone as I could get it, I did some weeding in the garden.

About three o'clock I heard the phone ring and I thought, not for the first time, that I should make a habit of bringing the phone outside when I was working there, because about half the time I didn't get inside before the rings stopped. This time, however, the caller was patient. I got to the phone and lifted the receiver.

It was a reporter calling about the shooting. The grapevine was alive and well. I told him we weren't giving interviews and hung up. The phone rang again.

I looked at it then picked it up.

A man's voice. "Mr. J. W. Jackson?"

"Yes."

"My name is Tom Rimini. I need your help."

4

"Carla sent me," said Rimini's voice. "Can we meet? I have your address, but I thought I should call first."

Several emotions, anger among them, tried to grip my tongue. I pushed them away. "Where are you?"

"I just got off the boat. I'm in Vineyard Haven."

"You have a car?"

"Yes. I'd have been here sooner, but I got caught in traffic last night and missed the late boat. And then I got stuck in the standby line most of the morning."

"Consider yourself lucky."

"What do you mean?"

"Two goons with guns came looking for you. You weren't here, but my wife and daughter were."

"Oh, my God! Are they all right?"

"They got banged around, but they'll be okay. You know how to get here from Vineyard Haven?"

"Well, I have directions, but . . ."

I told him how to do it. Pat and Howie had managed it on their own.

"Thanks."

"Don't thank me yet." I hung up, and went outside.

"Another stranger is coming," I said to the children. "Don't worry. He's not a bad guy. There won't be any more bad guys coming."

"I'm not scared," said brave Diana.

"Me neither," said Joshua.

"Good."

"Is it a man or a woman?"

"A man."

"What's his name?"

"Tom Rimini."

"I remember that name," said Diana. "The bad guys were looking for him, but he wasn't here."

"Well, he'll be here pretty soon. He and I are going to have a talk."

"Okay, Pa. Pa, can we have a dog?"

A dog? I didn't want a dog. We had two cats, Oliver Underfoot and Velcro, and that was enough animals.

"No, we can't have a dog," I said. "The cats wouldn't like one and I don't want to have to take care of one."

"We'll take care of it, Pa. Please?"

"No. No dog."

"Please, please?"

"No."

"All our friends have dogs."

"Fine. You can play with their dogs."

They put on their sniveling faces.

"Save your crying for when your mother gets home," I said. "It won't work with me."

"Can we have a fishpond with goldfish in it?"

A fishpond. That sounded interesting. You don't have to walk a fish or keep it on a leash.

"Maybe," I said.

Diana brightened. "Can I feed the goldfish, Pa?"

"No," said Joshua. "I want to feed the goldfish!"

"You can probably take turns," I said. "We won't decide until we build the pond and get the fish, and before we do that, we have to talk about it with your mother. She might not want to have a fishpond."

"Oh, she'll love one," said Joshua. "Ma loves fish!"

Zee certainly loved to catch and eat bluefish and bass and Spanish mackerel and other fish in Vineyard waters, but I didn't know if she'd love to have goldfish in a fishpond.

"We'll ask her tomorrow, when she comes home from the hospital," I said.

"Pa, can we have a ferret?"

"No ferrets! Now come and help me weed the garden. Be careful not to pull up any veggies."

We had just finished weeding when a green Honda came down the driveway and parked. A man got out. He was slender and looked pale and wan, as the poets used to say. He was about my age.

"Mr. Jackson?"

"Yes." I brushed off some dirt, and went to him.

He put out a clean hand. "I'm Tom Rimini."

It was a thin hand, and there were no calluses on it. A white-collar hand.

"Thanks for seeing me. I'm sure you don't have any idea why I'm here." He thought again. "Or maybe you do. Those men you mentioned . . ."

This was the man Carla had left me for. The sweet man who had a job that didn't require him to carry a gun or deal with the scum of the city. The man who, she could be sure, would come home to her safe and sound every night.

"I'm going to have a beer," I said. "You want one?"

"No. I . . ."

"We'll go up on the balcony," I said. "We can talk there. It's reserved for grown-ups.

Kids only get up with special permission." I pointed him at the stairs and went into the house for a bottle of Sam Adams, still America's best bottled beer, although the microbreweries were making some real contenders.

On the balcony I found Rimini looking out over the garden and Sengekontacket Pond to the barrier beach that ran between Edgartown and Oak Bluffs. There were cars parked along the beach road and beach umbrellas on their far side, where the waters of the sound slapped the shore. June people, trying to brown the meat in the Vineyard sun.

Rimini nodded his head. "It's a beautiful view. Carla still talks about it."

"She used to like to sit up here." I found a chair across the table from his. "What can I do for you, Mr. Rimini?"

"I'm in trouble." He rubbed his white hands together.

"I know. So are the people who know you. And some who don't."

"What do you mean? Oh. But you said your wife and daughter were all right. Your daughter looks fine. That's her down there, isn't it?"

"My wife and daughter will be fine. How long has it been since you talked with Carla?"

"Yesterday, just before I left to come down here. Why?"

"Where do you live, anyway?"

"Jamaica Plain. Why do you ask about Carla? Has something happened to her?" He put his upper teeth over his lower lip.

"Sometime after you left, some thugs had a talk with her. She told them you were here at my house. A couple of them came here looking for you this morning, but you weren't around. It pissed them off. If you left Jamaica Plain yesterday, what took you so long to get down here?"

"Is she all right? My God!" He stood up. "I need to use your phone!"

"Sit down." I had no sympathy for him. He hesitated, then sat. "Let's get to the issue," I said. "What did you do to Sonny Whelen to make him so mad at you?"

Rimini stared. "You know about Whelen?"

"He was in the Charlestown rackets when I was a cop in Boston. When Carla and I were still married. I see his name in *The Globe* now and then. Numbers, gambling, drugs, you name it. Why's he after you?"

Rimini looked down and rubbed his hands some more. "I owe him money. A lot of money. I don't have it."

It was a banal problem. Still, even gangsters normally didn't kill you if you owed them money. They might break your legs, or make you sell or sign over your property, but they preferred to keep you alive so you could pay them back. They were businessmen. Of course, they might kill you as a hint to other people who owed them money, but that wasn't the norm. You didn't kill the goose as long as it could still lay eggs.

"How much do you owe?" I asked.

He told me. I was impressed.

"I thought you taught in the public schools. How did you manage to get that far in the hole?"

"I do teach. We both do. We make enough money, but when we bought the house we bit off more than we could chew. We got behind in the mortgage payments and used credit cards. That made it worse. I took out some loans to pay off the cards and then couldn't pay back the loans. We were going to lose the house. One day I went over to Suffolk Downs. I'd never done that before, and I didn't know anything about racing, but I won. I liked it. I paid off some bills. It felt good. I went down to Rhode Island and played. I won some more for a while. You gamble, Mr. Jackson?"

"No." Although I like to play small-time poker and think I have a surefire method of winning at roulette, gambling mostly bores me.

"You're lucky," said Rimini. "It's just a way to have some fun for most people, but for others it's a sickness. I found out I'm one of the others. I couldn't stop. I bet on anything you can think of: sports, craps, anything. I found people who'd advance me money. When I lost it, I found somebody else who'd do it, and I'd pay back the first guy, or at least pay the interest. As long as they got the interest they didn't care."

"A one-man Ponzi scheme."

He nodded. "Yes. Carla didn't know for a long time, but finally I had to tell her. She told me to get help, but instead I went to a guy who, it turned out, works for Sonny Whelen. I had a hot streak and paid back most of what I owed, so this guy loaned me more when I asked for it. I had a tip on a race. A sure thing. All of it was to go on a long shot to show. The long shot tripped coming out of the gate."

"It must have been one hell of a tip for them to give that much dough to a school-teacher."

"A lot of people lost a lot of money when that horse fell. It was a very hot tip. I was in serious debt. The house was mortgaged to the maximum. Whelen wanted his money and I didn't have it and couldn't raise it. I got an idea. I went to him and offered to work for him in my school. There's a lot of gambling in schools and the money can add up. I'd work for nothing. He'd get all of the profits. So I did that. A little bookie game that got bigger. Teachers and students both. You have any idea how much money schoolkids have these days? A lot! I expanded. Got some people working for me in other schools. Whelen was happy. I was holding my own, paying vigorish and more."

"Sounds good. What happened?"

"One day a guy phoned me at my house. Said he wanted to see me in private. Said it was about Sonny Whelen." He hesitated. "We met in a café and he showed me a badge . . ."

"Let me guess," I said. "He told you he'd had his eye on you for quite a while. He knew all about your bookie business. He told you he was really after Sonny Whelen, and he needed somebody on the inside as a snitch, and that he had you in mind. He said that if you didn't do what he wanted, he was going to arrest you. Your career would be gone, your family would be in disgrace, and you would be in jail where, probably, you couldn't expect to live too long because

52

Sonny Whelen's got a long reach. How am I doing?"

"You're doing all right."

"Then he told you that if you cooperated things would go better for you. Less publicity, no jail, maybe a chance to move someplace else and start again. Whelen would be in jail where he couldn't get at you, nobody could collect the debt you owed him because the debt was illegal, justice and righteousness would prevail, and everybody but Sonny Whelen would live happily ever after."

Rimini nodded. "Something like that."

"And what did you tell him?"

"I told him I'd do it. And I did for most of this past year. Sonny got a kick out of having me working for him. He never got out of high school, and here he had a schoolteacher working for him. I was his pet pointy-headed intellectual. He even took Carla and me out to dinner a couple of times to show us off. The thing is, he was pretty casual about what he said to other people he was with, but they used names and terms I didn't know. Slang. I have a good memory, though, and afterward I wrote everything down, even if I didn't understand it, and gave it to Graham."

"Graham's the cop?"

"Yes. The words didn't make sense to me, but maybe they did to him. Maybe they steered the detectives in directions they wouldn't have gone otherwise. Graham was always glad to get them."

"And then what happened?"

Rimini rubbed his hands right on schedule. "And then somebody saw Graham talking with me and Sonny heard about it. Maybe Sonny was already beginning to have doubts about whether he could trust me. He didn't get where he is by trusting very many people, for sure. Anyway, a guy met me after school and took me to Sonny. I told him Graham was a gambler I owed money to. He said he'd never heard of a gambler by that name. I told him I didn't know if it was his real name. He said he didn't like me talking with Graham and to break it off. I went home and told Carla. It was two weeks before school let out, so I couldn't leave without attracting a lot of attention to myself. I was a wreck. I'd heard what gangsters do to stool pigeons."

I could imagine how he felt. He was between Scylla and Charybdis. "What did you do?"

"The next time Graham phoned I told him what had happened. He said to just be cool, but I didn't feel cool. Then I got the feeling somebody was watching me. Whenever I was out on the street, and sometimes when I was home. Somebody was out there in the shadows at night. I didn't know if I was imagining things or not. I finished the term, but I had to get away. Somewhere not too far away, where nobody knew me, where I could calm down and figure out what to do, where I'd be safe . . ."

"Someplace like here, where Carla loved to be because it was a long way from Boston and all the things about my job that scared her."

He met my stare. "Yes. She said to come here. She said you'd understand. She said she'd call you and talk with you and that it would be all right. She said I could trust you, and that you could help me. But she never called, did she?"

"No."

"They did something bad to her, didn't they? Otherwise, she'd have called. Otherwise, she never would have told them where I was going. Jesus." He stood up. "I've got to go back."

It was a simple solution to my own problems. Rimini would be out of my hair and I wouldn't have to give another thought to Sonny Whelen. I should have said nothing. Instead, I said, "Wait a minute."

5

He turned back to me.

"Let me make some phone calls first," I said. "You're as safe here as anyplace else for the moment, because they've already looked here and learned the hard way it was the wrong house."

"I'm not interested in being safe. I'm interested in Carla and the kids!" He started down the stairs. I went after him and caught him before he got to his car.

"Look," I said. "You're not going to do anybody any good by barging back up to Jamaica Plain. If Whelen really is after you, you'll be walking right into his arms. Carla and the kids don't need a dead dad, they need a live one."

"But she may be hurt! And what about the kids?!"

"A couple of phone calls will tell us what happened. . . . Maybe Carla just got scared into talking. Not every hood beats up women the way Pat Logan liked to do. Where do your folks live?"

"Brookline."

"Fine. Carla's are in Milton. If Carla's not

at home, she and the kids will probably be in one of those two places."

"I don't like this."

"You've made yourself a bed of nails. Now you've got to lie on it. You come in and sit down and I'll make the calls."

He wasn't a fool, even though he had been acting like one for quite a while. He stared at the ground like a teenager caught shoplifting a stuffed toy for his girlfriend. Then he nodded. "Okay. But if she's hurt, I'm going up there!"

And do what? I wondered. "Come into the house," I said. "We'll call your place first. What's the number?"

He told me and I dialed. The voice that answered was agitated but so familiar that my heart did a little turn.

"Carla, this is Jeff. How are you?"

I could hear her take a deep breath and let it out. "Jeff. I'm fine. How . . . how are you?"

"Are you alone? Can you talk?"

"Yes. I meant to phone you, Jeff. I . . ."

"Listen to me, Carla. It's important. First, Tom is fine. He's in a safe place."

"Oh, thank God! If anything happened to him . . ."

"Never mind that, now. Some guys visited you and you told them Tom would be at my place. Did they hurt you or did they just scare you into telling them?"

"They didn't hurt me. I'm not brave, I guess. They know where my kids go to school. They told me about accidents that happen to people. Is Tom really all right?"

"Yes."

"I'm sorry I told him to go down there, but it was the only place I could think of. He was scared! I was going to call you and tell you he was coming, but it was like those men could read my mind! They told me not to call anybody! That they'd know, if I did. That they'd be back. Is Tom there with you? Let me talk with him!"

"I'll have him call you later. It's better that you don't know where he is, because those guys may be back for the information."

"I wouldn't tell them! Not again!"

Maybe; maybe not. "You can't tell what you don't know," I said. "Right now all you need to know is that he's in a safe spot. I'll have him get in touch with you later, so the two of you can talk. How are your children?"

"They're fine. We're fine. They're getting ready to go play tennis. Is that safe? Should I let them go? God, Jeff, I feel like I did when you were on the police force. I'm scared all the time!" I could hear the fear in her voice. It was a familiar tone that I remembered well from the last years of our marriage.

She was not frightened without cause. "I don't think you need to be afraid," I lied. "They're not going to hurt you or your children, and your husband is safe and sound. We'll figure a way out of this mess."

"I wish he were home! I wish none of this had happened!"

I felt the same helpless wave of pity for her that I'd felt long, long ago, when she had wished that I was someone other than who I was, and did something other than what I did, when we had loved each other but couldn't live together anymore.

"He'll get home," I said. "Meanwhile, you have to be tough. We'll work it out."

"I'm not tough, Jeff. If I was tough I never would have left you."

I remembered the scene in the Boston hospital. I was sitting on a bed, bandages on my belly where the bullet had entered and the surgeons had gone in to do repairs but had left the slug nestled against my spine because leaving it there was less dangerous than trying to dig it out. Carla was going out the door, her head bowed, her light brown hair neatly combed as always. She had just told me that she was divorcing me. She was crying. So was I.

"Women are always tougher than men," I

said. "I'll have your husband call you later."

Before she could say anything else, I hung up the phone.

Rimini was looking at me. "Well?"

"She's fine. The kids are fine. Whelen's goons scared her, but they didn't hurt her."

"You should have let me talk with her." He reached for the phone.

I stopped his clean white hand with my rough tan one. "No. If you talk with her now, she'll know you're here. If she knows, Whelen can know. We'll wait. You can call her in an hour or two. She won't know where you are, and you won't tell her. Not if you want to stay safe."

"Safe! What good does it do for me to be safe? I've got to get out of this mess!"

I almost felt sorry for him. He was stewing in his own juice.

"It took you time to get into it," I said. "It may take some to get you out of it. While we work at it you park your gear in that spare room there."

"I can't leave Carla and the kids alone!"

He irked me. "The best thing you can do for your wife and family is disappear for a while, till we work things out. You're an amateur in this sort of game. I know a little more about it, so let me see what I can do."

"You're right." He rubbed a hand over his

hair. "I don't know what to do or how to do it. Do you really think you can do something?" Then a bitter note entered his voice. "And if you can, why should you?"

Why, indeed? Because of the Riminis, my wife was in the hospital and my daughter had been cut by a knifeman. The Riminis had brought me nothing but grief. But I had once loved Carla.

"Because I'm already involved," I said. "Sonny Whelen thinks I know where you are. Worse yet, he's lost a couple of his men here at my house, and he won't be happy about that when he finds out. I have to get him out of my life."

He nodded, but then gave me a nervous look. "You could do that by just handing me over to him. I couldn't complain if you did."

I liked him a little better for saying that. "I don't usually hand people over to thugs."

"Not even me?"

"Especially you."

"Why?"

"Because I used to be married to your wife. I don't want to help make her a widow. You can stay here tonight while I think about a better place for you to hang out."

He eyed me thoughtfully, then nodded. "I'll get my gear." He went out.

I went into the bedroom and used that

61

phone to call Quinn. Quinn is a reporter for *The Boston Globe*. I'd met him when I was a cop up there, and we'd hit it off. When I needed to know something about who was who and what was what in Massachusetts, I still called Quinn.

He answered on the first ring, which meant he was writing up a story. Otherwise, he was almost never at his desk.

"I'll trade you a story for some information," I said.

"I usually come out on the short end of these deals with you," said Quinn, "but I'll do it for your wife's sake. She's stuck with you when she really wants me."

"As a matter of fact, the story is about Zee. It's too good not to get out pretty fast, so since I feel sorry for you for being such a dud as a reporter, I thought I'd try to save your career by offering it to you first."

"Speak."

I told him the tale as I'd heard it, omitting only Tom Rimini's name.

"Wow! That's good," said Quinn happily. "I can see the headline now: GANGLAND GUNMEN MEET THEIR MATCH; SMALL-TOWN HOUSEWIFE MOWS THEM DOWN. Or something like that. I think I got everything but the name of the guy they were after."

Sharp Quinn. "You didn't get it because I didn't give it to you."

"Don't be coy. I can get it somewhere else. Some cop will tell me."

True. "Off the record, then."

"Okay. But if I get it someplace else, I'll feel free to use it."

"Fair enough. They were after a guy named Tom Rimini. He's a schoolteacher with a gambling habit." I told him Rimini's tale. When I was through, I added: "I want to keep him out of the story as much as possible, because I want to get him out from under Sonny Whelen's thumb if I can."

I could almost see Quinn's ears perk up. "How come this interest in Mr. Rimini? You old buddies, or something? He save your life in Nam or some such thing, like in the movies?"

"Nothing like that. He's married to Carla."

"Ah." Then, "So?"

A good question. I gave him the only answer I'd come up with: "She lost one husband, me, and I don't want her to lose another one. She doesn't deserve that."

There was a silence. Then he said, "Okay, I guess. I don't want to belabor the obvious, but aren't you married to Zee now? How long has it been since you've even seen Carla?"

"A lot of years."

"You still think you owe her?" Quinn was a bachelor who had had a lot of women in his life. I wondered if he even remembered them all.

"I guess I just don't want to see her get hurt anymore."

"Zee know about all this?"

"Not yet. She might tomorrow, if she gets home and finds Rimini still here in our spare room."

"What? You're keeping him there at your place?"

"For the night, at least. Hey, maybe I can send him up to your place instead? Nobody would think of looking for him there."

"Very funny. I have one bedroom and I don't share it with men. No, you keep him."

"And you keep that detail out of your story. Now, here's what you can do for me in exchange for me spilling my guts to you."

"What?"

"Two things: check on the cop named Graham. The one who turned Rimini. I want to know as much about him as you can dig up. Who he's working for, and all that."

"Don't you trust Graham?"

"I don't trust him or not trust him. Before

I do either, I want to know as much as I can about him.

"Second, I want you to find out where I can meet Sonny Whelen. I want to talk with him."

"Oh, no, you don't," said Quinn. "No, no, no. Sonny is going to be in a bad mood when he hears about what happened to his lads this morning."

"He's not the only one in a bad mood," I said. "Find out where he lives, where he likes to eat, and where he hangs out. When I was pounding the streets up in Bean Town, Sonny was out and about in Charlestown, like he owned the place."

"Which he pretty much did, and still does, although that idea might be challenged by Pete McBride. Pete is beginning to think he should run the rackets in Charlestown."

"Fine. Maybe they'll shoot each other and my problems will be solved. Meanwhile, if you have any contacts with Sonny's associates, tell them that I want to meet with him. Tell them that he can name the time and place, but that I want it to happen soon."

"J.W., I'm telling you that I don't think that is a good idea."

"Just do it, please."

"All right. But I don't like it."

"Look on the bright side," I said. "If anything happens to me you'll have a clean shot at Zee. Of course, you'll have to convince her first that a reporter is an actual human being. It won't be easy."

I had no sooner hung up the phone than it rang. It was a reporter from the Cape. I told him that the Jacksons weren't home and rang off. In the guest room, Rimini was looking at the decoys my father had carved so long ago.

"Those are very nice," he said.

"Sit down," I said. "Just so you don't change your mind about running home to save Carla, I want you to know what happened here this morning."

He sat, and I told him. He looked sick when I was through.

6

An hour later, Rimini and I and the kids got into the old Toyota and I drove him down to the parking lot at the foot of Edgartown's Main Street. There are some public telephones there on the side of what used to be the Junior Yacht Club building. Now the Junior Yacht Club has snazzier quarters, although they're nothing in comparison to the senior Yacht Club. There were a lot of summer people and cars on the streets, but fate was kind and we actually found a parking place right where we wanted one.

We went to the phones and while Joshua and Diana ogled the boats tied to the dock, I handed a receiver to Rimini.

"There's a possibility that the phone at your house has been tapped, or the house itself might be bugged. Probably neither of those things has happened, but they might have. So for the next few days, when you call your wife, always use a public phone and never tell her or anyone else where you're staying."

"My house bugged? My telephone tapped? Who would do anything like that?"

67

The idea seemed to astonish Rimini.

"I can think of two people," I said. "Sonny Whelen and Graham. Both because they'd want to know who you meet and what you say when you're out of their sight."

"My God! Do you really think it's possible?"

It was easy for me to be impatient with him. I shrugged. "I think it's unlikely, but I think you should act like it was true. You decide. It's your life."

He shook his head and turned to the phone.

"And you might skip what happened at my house this morning," I said. "That might scare Carla more than she needs to be."

I stepped away, but not too far away because I didn't know if I could trust him to be discreet. I looked past the yacht club, but my ears were aimed at the bank of phones.

More and more boats, both sail and power, were coming into the harbor and finding moorings as July drew nearer. The *Shirley J.*, our eighteen-foot Herrishoff America, was swinging on her stake halfway between the yacht club and the Reading Room dock, where she had been moored since early May. She was a lovely thing, and as usual when I looked at her, I felt the old urge to stop whatever I was doing and go sailing for a few days. I'd been able to drop everything and do stuff like that when I'd been a bachelor, but now I was a married man with a family, so I had to keep myself more in check. It wasn't hard to opt for Zee and the kids, but any sailboat was still a siren.

Right now, of course, I had Rimini and Sonny Whelen to deal with, so there'd be no sailing for me. Not for a while.

Off to my left, Rimini's voice spoke of love and caring and regret and loneliness and the hope, but not the promise, of coming home. When at last he hung up the phone, Rimini looked tired and sad.

"Come on, kids," I said. "Let's get some ice cream and then head for home." I glanced at Rimini. "You, too. Ice cream is good for you whether you have troubles or not."

Rimini tried a smile. "Maybe you're right."

So we walked up to North Water Street, bought and ate four separate flavors, then drove back to the house.

The next morning I was feeding blueberry pancakes to the children when Rimini came into the kitchen. He didn't look like he'd had the good night's sleep that doctors recommend.

I waved a spatula. "There's juice in the fridge and coffee right there. Help yourself. Pancakes coming up."

He went straight for the coffee. I wasn't surprised because I've been told that for schoolteachers, like cops and doctors, coffee and booze are the fluids of choice.

I put a plate of pancakes in front of him. "Eat. These are our own berries off our own bushes out back. We picked them last year."

"Pa," said Joshua. "I'm done."

I eyed him. He looked pretty sticky. "Okay. Go wash the syrup off your hands and face."

He climbed off his chair and I looked at Diana the Huntress. Unlike her big brother, Diana seemed far from done. She lifted her eyes from her empty plate.

"More, Pa?"

"Sure, sweetie."

I served her another pancake. Like her mother, Diana could eat a horse and never seem to gain an ounce.

By the time Joshua reappeared to show me his now fairly clean hands and face, Diana, too, announced that she was done. If possible, she was even more syrupy than her brother had been. I took her into the bathroom and helped her scrub. Joshua followed.

"When are we going to get Ma?"

"Soon. You two go play for a while. I want to talk with Mr. Rimini."

"Why can't we stay and listen?"

"Because it's private big-people talk."

"So?"

"So me no so's. You two go out and play. When I finish talking with Mr. Rimini, we'll go for a ride and bring your mother home."

The carrot did it. "Okay, Pa. Come on, Diana."

I went back into the kitchen and got myself some pancakes. The cook is often last to eat. They were worth waiting for.

"I'm going to move you to another house," I said to Rimini, between mouthfuls. "The police and the D.A. will be wanting to talk with my wife and if they find you here they may make your life more complicated than it already is. Ours, too. It's also possible that one of them may let it slip that you're here and that Whelen may get the news. I don't want any of his goons coming here, ever."

He chewed and swallowed, then nodded. "Makes sense."

"I take care of a house that belongs to some friends of mine. John and Mattie Skye, and their twin daughters. John teaches up at Weststock College. They usually summer

71

here, but right now the whole family is out in Colorado where his kin still live. They won't be back on the island until August, so the house is empty. It's off the road, so you'll have as much privacy as you need, and John's got a huge library, so you won't get bored. I called John this morning and told him I wanted to put an extra guest of mine in his house for a few days. He said it was okay, so I'm going to give you a map and a key. You pick up some groceries and go on out there. Call me later this morning after you get moved in, but don't call your wife from that phone because the call might be traced. And don't tell her where you are. She can't tell anybody else what she doesn't know."

"I'm sorry I brought this to you."

"You didn't. Carla did. Of course, you brought it to her, and of course, neither of you meant to have it happen. But now we have to try to get you out of it. I'll see what I can do. Meanwhile, you go play hermit at John Skye's house, and don't tell anybody anything they don't need to know."

"You don't need to do this. You don't owe me anything."

"I have a bone of my own to pick with Sonny Whelen. His goons hurt my wife and daughter, and I plan to have a talk with him about that."

He seemed to shrink in size. "Maybe I should just go back and face the consequences."

"If you want Carla to be a widow or maybe the wife of a cripple, maybe you should do that. You're grown up, so you can do as you please." I dug an envelope out of a pocket and handed it to him. "This is a map to John Skye's place and the key to his front door. I think you'd be smart to just hang out there for a while, but it's up to you."

He seemed to be through eating, so I finished off my pancakes and stacked the dishes in the sink while he sat over his coffee cup and thought about his options. I felt both sympathy and impatience.

"I'm going up to the hospital to pick up Zee. You decide what you're going to do."

He looked up at me and nodded. "I will. And thanks."

"I haven't done anything yet," I said, and went out.

A half hour later, the children and I were at the hospital. There was a TV van in the parking lot. I drove past and we went into the building and came out again by a far door. By ten we were all home again. Rimini was gone with all his gear.

Zee was bruised but uncomplaining. Still, the rest of us treated her as if she were made of glass.

"Here, Ma. Sit down here," said Joshua, leading her to her favorite chair.

Zee eased down. "Thank you, Josh."

Oliver Underfoot and Velcro, the cats, wandered in and joined the family.

"Here's Bear," said Diana. "You can hold her."

Zee smiled a split-lipped smile, and took Bear. "Oh, thank you, Diana."

"Pa says we shouldn't climb on you for a while," said Joshua.

I leaned over and whispered in her ear. "I was saving the climbing for myself."

"What'd you say, Pa?"

"Nothing, Josh."

"When will you be better, Ma?"

"Soon. I'm almost better right now."

"You got a black eye, Ma."

She nodded, smiling. "It'll go away."

"And you have a bloody lip."

She ran her tongue over it. "It will get better soon."

"I had a split lip once."

"More than once, as I recall, Diana."

Joshua came out of the guest room. "That man is gone, Pa."

"Yes. He was just here for the night."

Zee looked at me. "What man?"

"Tom Rimini."

She frowned and then waited for an explanation.

"Let's all go out in the yard," I said. "It's a beautiful day." I put out my hands and helped Zee to her feet.

She and I sat on lawn chairs and sure enough, just as I had hoped, Joshua and Diana were soon too busy playing to listen to me talk with their mother. I told her everything I knew about Rimini and everything that had happened between him and me. She listened well.

When I was through, she thought for a while, then nodded. "So those men came here because your ex-wife sent them here."

"Yes."

"Women!" she snapped. But then she took a breath, grimacing as she did. "Well, I might have done the same thing, I guess. In fact I probably would have told them anything they wanted to know, or done anything they wanted me to do. I tried to do that yesterday, in fact, but they didn't believe me. I had that pistol but she didn't have one. I guess I can't blame her." She put a hand to her side, where Pat Logan's bullet had creased her. "I'll be glad when I'm back to normal."

"I'm just glad you're here at all."

"Me, too!" She put out her hand and I took it.

The phone rang, and I looked at Joshua. "Go answer that, will you? If somebody needs to talk with your mother or me, bring it out here."

"Okay, Pa."

Joshua galloped into the house and out again.

"It's for you, Pa."

I was ready for another reporter, but Tom Rimini was on the other end of the line. He had decided to hole up in the Skyes' house. I told him that I thought that was wise, that I'd be back in touch, and that there were reporters and TV crews on the island, so it might be smart of him to stay out of sight.

"What are your plans for him?" asked Zee, as I laid the phone on the grass beside my chair. "He can't hide out forever."

"My plans are to take care of me and mine first. After that, I'll worry about him and his. I'm going up to Boston tomorrow and have a talk with Sonny Whelen, if I can find him."

Her hand tightened in mine. "No. We don't want any more trouble with Sonny Whelen."

"Don't worry," I said. "I don't plan to get

into any trouble. In fact, I want to make sure that our paths won't cross again." I felt a crooked smile appear on my face as I looked at her. "I think Sonny may agree to a peace treaty. He hasn't fared too well with the Jacksons so far."

Zee took her hand away from mine. "I still have a hard time believing that really happened."

"It really happened, and you did absolutely the right thing."

But Zee's face wore a cloud of doubt.

7

One of the perks of being an official resident of Martha's Vineyard is that sometimes you get first dibs on round-trip reservations off and then back onto the island. Because of this, and because in late June more people are trying to get onto the island than off it, I was aboard an early ferry to Woods Hole the next morning.

I stood on the deck and watched the Vineyard grow smaller astern as the Elizabeth Islands and the Cape grew larger ahead. There weren't many sailboats out yet, so there was little to see but water and seagulls riding the gentle morning wind. It was going to be another beautiful day on the beautiful island of Martha's Vineyard, but I was headed for Boston and didn't expect to encounter much loveliness during my day.

It took me two hours to get to the *Globe* building, thanks to the morning rush-hour traffic jam, which, as usual, consisted of more jam than rush, and it was once again clear to me that Edgartown's infamous A&P/Al's Package Store traffic jam, about which I complained a great deal, was nothing compared to what Route 128 and the expressways into Boston had to offer. How intelligent you were, J.W., to have swapped city life for island life.

I found Quinn a few desks away from his own, talking with a sportswriter. They were arguing about the Red Sox, the principal bone of contention apparently being whether the current management of the team was the stupidest in history or merely the stupidest in the past decade. Quinn, who made a point of being a natty dresser to belie the notion that all reporters were slobs, was in considerable sartorial contrast to his jeans-and-sweatshirt-wearing colleague.

Quinn was ticking off the names of departed players on his fingers. "First, of course, there was Ruth. The Sox haven't won a World Series since they gave him to the Yankees; then there was Fisk, the best catcher in baseball; then just in the nineties alone they said Roger was past his prime and wouldn't pay up to keep him, and all he did was win the Cy Young Award the next two years; and they said Canseco wasn't producing and let him go, and all he did was hit forty home runs the next year; and then they let Mo, their best player, go, after his best year in the majors! And then they have the gall to raise ticket prices up to the moon.

You tell me. Is this any way to run a professional baseball team? Hi, J.W."

"What a golden tongue you have, Quinn," said the sportswriter. "You should come over to our side of the room and write sports news." He smiled at me.

"Shake hands with Jack Thorn," said Quinn. "He's conned the editors of this mighty metropolitan newspaper into paying him to watch grown men playing kids' games. Jack, this is J. W. Jackson, who does nothing but loaf and fish on the Vineyard. Worse yet, he's married to a beautiful woman who's really in love with me."

Jack and I shook hands. "Nice to meet you," said Thorn. "Well, I got a story to write, and I have to make some calls first." He walked to a nearby desk, sat down, and reached for the phone.

Quinn led me to his own desk. "I presume that you haven't gotten any smarter than when we talked before. I was hoping you'd changed your mind or had second thoughts about meeting Whelen. How are Zee and your daughter?"

Images of Zee's bruised face and Diana's bandaged throat appeared in my mind. "They'll be all right. Did you find out what I want to know?"

"Yeah, I found Sonny Whelen at least. It wasn't hard."

"What about Graham?"

"Not yet. You want half a loaf, or none?"

"I'll take the half you got."

"Okay. Charlestown is like a castle for Sonny Whelen. It's his private fortress. He goes where he pleases and does what he pleases. He's right out in the open as often as he wants to be, but he doesn't have to worry about the cops or anybody else, because half the townies look out for him. Nobody can get close to him unless he wants them to. They should call him King Whelen. Of course, uneasy lies the crowned head, even in Charlestown. Pete McBride, as I believe I mentioned, apparently aspires to the throne."

"Tell me about Pete McBride."

"A courtier, you might say."

"The man who would be king?"

"Yes, but Pete isn't big enough to make any moves on Sonny, not that he wouldn't like to. Someday, maybe, but not yet. He may be hatching plans, but he's not ready to make his play."

"Lord Peter and King Sonny. How Shakespearean. Maybe you should write a play. How can I see Whelen?"

Quinn tapped his fingers on his desk.

"You can't see him. Not alone. You sure you want to go through with this?"

"I'm sure. How can I do it?"

Quinn sighed. "By going with me. I know Whelen. I even interviewed him once. Wrote his side of things. Series we ran on police corruption. He denied being any kind of criminal, of course."

"I remember."

"I quoted him straight, and he appreciated that. He knows I'm not his pet reporter, but he also knows he'll get a square deal from me. I've talked with a couple of his flunkies. Told them I had a friend who wants a few words with Sonny. Asked them to tell Whelen."

"And?"

"He likes to eat lunch at the Green Harp. It's a brewpub up by the monument. You Irish?"

"On St. Patrick's Day, at least."

"You dressed? If you are, shed it here. You can pick it up when you go home. I won't take you if you're carrying."

"No. No gun. I'm not planning on shooting anybody. All I want to do is talk."

"Good. Last chance, now; you're really sure you want to do this?"

"Yes."

He tapped his fingers some more, then

looked at his watch, picked up his phone, and dialed a number.

"This is Quinn, over at *The Globe*. Tell Mr. Whelen that the friend I mentioned and I are heading over to have a beer and some lunch in the Green Harp, and that we'd like to buy him a Guinness. Yeah, that's right: Quinn."

He hung up and grabbed his hat and we went out. As we drove toward the river, Quinn spoke of our destination and of Sonny Whelen.

Charlestown is a part of Boston that I never worked in while I was a cop. It lies on a hilly little peninsula between the Charles and the Mystic rivers, and is where Paul Revere waited to see one light or two before setting out on his famous ride. It's also the site of the Bunker Hill Monument, built to celebrate the battle where, according to legend, the Colonials waited to see the whites of the British regulars' eyes before firing. The facts that the battle was really fought on nearby Breed's Hill and that the British won have not diminished the renown of the monument, which remains a popular tourist attraction.

Charlestown is also the home of a fine community college; the birthplace of Samuel Morse, inventor of the telegraph;

the site of John Harvard's grave; and the home of a lot of decent, ordinary people.

It is, however, better known nowadays to Massachusetts cops and D.A.'s for the affinity of its mobsters to rob banks and armored cars, and the three monkeys' attitude of many of its citizens toward local criminals. If you are set upon a life of crime, there are worse places to live than Charlestown, as certain genealogical evidence proves, for in Charlestown it was not rare for members of two or even three generations of the same family to be concurrently serving time for similar crimes.

Sonny Whelen's people had been in the rackets for a hundred years, ever since they'd come over from County Cork, but Sonny was the first to achieve major league status and was, therefore, a subject of no little pride to his kith and kin and, to only a slightly lesser extent, to townspeople who could bask in the reflected glow of his fame. He further ensured his popularity by the time-honored practice of giving generously to local charities, aiding widows and orphans, and making sure that the streets were safe for civilians. Sonny's mob might be tough and frightening, but few people outside of the profession they practiced were ever killed or damaged in Charlestown. Beyond Charlestown, of course, such was not the case, as many guards of banks and armored cars could attest, if they were still alive. Still, like many successful criminals, Sonny preferred to practice nonviolence whenever possible, since killings always roused passions and therefore increased the dangers of retaliation from the relatives and friends of the victims, and might also goad the authorities into action they might otherwise not take.

There are a lot of narrow streets in Charlestown, and on one of them I found a place to park my car. We walked about two blocks and came to the Green Harp, another one of the many new brewpubs that are springing up all over the country and which, I believe, offer the best evidence we have that the nation is not, after all, going to the dogs, but is actually improving. All that microbrewery beer suggests a future full of hope.

We went inside. It was just before noon, and the place was about half full. The bar curved out in a semicircle from the back wall. Booths lined the side walls, and there were tables in the front. The farthest corner of the room was beyond my sight. I ignored the many eyes I felt upon us and the falling away of voices as the regulars took note of us

— two strangers — and followed Quinn to the bar.

"Two pints of Guinness, if you please."

The wide-bodied bartender pulled the drinks and put them before us. I paid and touched my glass to Quinn's. We drank the good, dark, smooth, strong Guinness, and ordered another.

"There's a booth," I said. "Shall we sit?"

"Patience," said Quinn.

I drank some more Guinness.

A man appeared beside Quinn, a glass in his hand. "Is this your friend, Mr. Quinn?" He leaned forward over the bar and peeked at me. I peeked back.

"This is him," said Quinn. "Mr. Jackson."

"Mr. Jackson, perhaps you'll step into the gents for a moment?"

"Why not?"

Another man was in the rest room when we went in. He just stood there, looking at me. He didn't seem to be there to use the facilities. The place was amazingly clean, unlike most of the heads I've seen in bars.

"Nothing personal, you understand," said the first man. He patted me down briskly but thoroughly. "What's this?"

"Pocketknife." I brought it out. He waved it back.

"All right, then," he said. "Come on."

We went out and he led me to the last booth along the far wall. There was a door between the booth and the bar, and a waiter came out carrying a platter of good-smelling pub grub. Quinn was sitting in the booth across from two other men. One of them looked to be about fifty. He had an Irish face and very pale hair, eyes, and eyebrows. The man beside him was slim and expressionless and kept his hands out of sight under the table. I sat down beside Quinn, and the man who'd led me there went away. I didn't think he'd gone far.

"This is my friend J. W. Jackson, the guy I told you about," said Quinn.

"What do you want?" asked the man with pale hair.

"First, I'd like to buy you a Guinness, if you're Sonny Whelen," I said.

The man beside the pale man looked at me. "You some kind of a joker?"

"Easy, Todd," said the pale man.

"I've never seen Sonny Whelen," I said to both men. "I don't want to talk with his twin or his stand-in, I want to talk with him." I turned to Quinn. "Is this him?"

"It's him," said Quinn. "Would a newspaperman lie?"

"Fine." I looked back at Whelen. "Then, can I buy you that drink?"

Whelen smiled. "Okay, Mr. Jackson." He made a small gesture and a waiter appeared. "Three Guinnesses, Mike." The waiter disappeared and Whelen nodded toward the man beside him, who was looking steadily at me. "Todd, here, don't drink while he's on the job. Do you, Todd?"

"No," said Todd.

Three pints of Guinness were deposited on our table and we drank.

"Now," said Whelen, "what is it you want to talk about, Mr. Jackson?"

I held my glass in one hand and put my other hand flat on the table where Whelen and Todd could both see that it was empty.

"The day before yesterday," I said, "two guys who work for you, Pat Logan and Howie Trucker, came to my house on Martha's Vineyard looking for a guy named Tom Rimini. I wasn't there, but my wife and little daughter were. My wife told them that Rimini wasn't there and that she'd never heard of him, which was true, but they didn't believe her. Trucker put a knife to my daughter's throat, and Logan beat my wife and was about to beat her some more. But that didn't happen because she killed Logan and shot Trucker to pieces. I want to know what you had to do with it."

8

No one spoke. Then Whelen's eyes narrowed.

"Do you know where you are?"

"I'm sitting in a pub talking with a man who says he's Sonny Whelen, but I never heard of Sonny Whelen sending strong-arm men to cut little girls' throats and beat up women. Or did I hear wrong?"

"Sonny, you don't have to put up with this shit," said Todd.

"Be quiet," said Whelen. He looked at Quinn. "Did you know this was why he wanted to see me?"

Quinn shook his head. "No, I didn't. But maybe I should have guessed." He touched my shoulder. "Come on, J.W., let's ease out of here before you make any more friends. Is that okay, Sonny?"

"Wait," said Whelen. The pale eyes switched back to me. "Your wife killed The Pilot? You're the guy who owns the house?"

"That's right, and that's why I'm here. I don't like trouble, and I don't want any more of it. From you or anybody else."

The tension went out of Whelen's face.

He picked up his glass and drank.

"You must be married to some kind of woman. The Pilot was a pretty tough guy, they say. The papers are making quite a lot out of it. The Pilot shot down while attacking civilians, and stuff like that." He glanced at Quinn.

"I don't write the headlines," said Quinn. "Just the stories."

"People are having a lot of laughs," said Whelen. "Gunmen outgunned by mother of two. Big-city mobsters pick on the wrong country girl. Cute. I even seen the story on television. If I was the crime boss that some people think I am, I might be pretty pissed off to have people laughing at my gang like that. It's not good for business to have people laugh at you. Of course, I'm not a crime boss, and I barely even knew those two guys, so you're talking to the wrong man, Mr. Jackson."

"Not according to Howie Trucker. I managed to have a chat with him before they flew him up here to the hospital. Howie said you sent them to find Rimini."

Whelen turned to Todd. "Howie Trucker. Ain't he the famous liar? The crook that's never told the truth in his life?"

"Yeah," said Todd. "That's him."

Whelen turned back to me. "This

90

Trucker guy has been bad-mouthing me for years. Every time he does something illegal he tries to blame me for it. I don't know what's wrong with him. I guess he's sick or something. Maybe he got kicked by a horse or something when he was a kid."

"Maybe," I said.

"So I guess we got nothing to talk about, Mr. Jackson. Sounds like those bums your wife shot got what was coming to them."

"I think so. Here's the thing, Mr. Whelen. Maybe you sent those goons down there to find Rimini, and maybe you didn't, but you're said to be an influential man in these parts, so you can do me a favor by spreading the word that I want no more Charlestown muscle in my life, ever. I want me and mine to be left alone. You do that and we're square. We'll write off what happened as just a mistake made by a couple of wiseguys on their own."

Whelen sipped his Guinness, and smiled. "And what if I don't spread the word?"

"I'll be unhappy."

"So what?" said Todd.

I didn't look at him. I looked into Sonny's snowy eyes.

Sonny turned his glass on the table, making small damp circles. "You'll be unhappy, eh? Are you hinting that you're

91

dangerous when you're unhappy, Mr. Jackson?"

"Unhappy people are always more dangerous than happy ones," I said. "You know that. But you don't have to worry about me. You're surrounded by people who are more dangerous to you than I'll ever be."

Sonny studied me without expression, then he said, "You say your wife never heard of Rimini. You ever hear of him?"

"Of course I've heard of him," I said, telling him what I was sure he already knew. "Carla, my first wife, left me and married him. He's a schoolteacher. When things started to pile up on him, Carla remembered the place where we used to vacation on the Vineyard and told him to hide out there with me. Then she got squeezed by your toughs and told them what she'd told Rimini. The thing is, she never told me anything. Maybe she planned to, but she never did; anyway, your goons showed up before he did."

The pale eyes brightened. "You telling me that Rimini's there now?"

"No." I leaned forward. "Rimini showed up that afternoon. After talking to him and to my ex on the phone I finally got the picture. She said she sent him to my house because it was the safest place she could think of. But all she'd brought me was grief, and I didn't want him there, so I sent him on his way. I'd had enough of Tom Rimini's problems."

"Where is he now?"

Time to lie. "I don't know."

"Don't you now? All right, where might he have gone?"

"I advised him to go to the cops."

He looked at me with those white-ice eyes. "And did he do that?"

I looked back. "I don't know what he did or where he went. But I know this: he's not at my house and I want no more of him or of you."

"Well, Mr. Jackson, we don't always get what we want, do we? There are some people here in town, for instance, who want to see Tom Rimini and probably won't stop looking until they find him. Those people will take it bad if they find out people have been sheltering him and lying about it."

"So far," I said, "all Tom Rimini has been to me is trouble. I moved to Martha's Vineyard to get away from trouble."

"You want to know a funny thing?" asked Whelen. "I hear that The Pilot and Howie Trucker didn't go down there to find Rimini. I hear that they were already there, on vacation with their wives in a place

Trucker owns down there. Not a bad place. I was down there once or twice myself. I hear that they got a call from Boston or somewhere and went over to collect Rimini as a sort of favor before they went to the beach. What do you think of that? You never know what's going to happen, do you? You're on vacation, you're going to the beach, then you do a friend a favor and you end up dead."

"Even Attila the Hun probably went on vacation," I said, "and we all end up dead sooner or later. But Howie Trucker's not dead yet. I imagine the cops will want to keep him alive so he can talk to them."

"Fuck Howie Trucker," said Todd.

"The Pilot was a stupid man," said Whelen. "His brain was in his crotch. I hear that Howie was supposed to keep him in line on this caper, but I guess he didn't do his job. Your wife a looker, Mr. Jackson?"

I saw the bruises on her face. "Yes."

He nodded. "Yeah. Well, The Pilot never could keep his hands off a good-looking woman." His glacier eyes bored into mine. "Whoever sent him made a mistake. People make mistakes."

I thought it was as near as I was going to get to an admission of error.

"Yeah," I said. "I guess The Pilot paid for

his own, and for the one made by whoever sent him. I don't want any more mistakes."

"Yeah," said Whelen. He sat back. "Well, thanks for the drink, Mr. Jackson. See you around, Mr. Quinn."

I got up and Quinn slid out of the booth and stood beside me.

"One other thing," said Whelen, looking up at me.

"What's that?"

"You sure you don't know where Rimini is?"

"I know where he isn't. He isn't at my house, and I don't want any more wiseguys looking for him there."

He cocked his head to one side. "Don't try to be too smart or too tough, Mr. Jackson. It's not healthy. You happen to run into Tom Rimini, you tell him to go home. Tell him his friends miss him."

"I'm hungry," I said to Quinn, "but I've changed my mind about having pub grub. Take me to the nearest Big Mac."

"Sure," said Quinn, and we walked out of the Green Harp feeling Irish eyes on our backs.

"You're terrific," said Quinn. "You should take up politics. You're a born diplomat. You're lucky Todd didn't shoot your balls off."

"I doubt if anybody does much shooting in the Green Harp," I said. "Sonny likes a nice Irish bar and likes to keep his own life quiet and peaceful. Todd probably does his shooting somewhere else, when Sonny isn't around. Was Pete McBride there just now?"

"Yeah. Chunky fellow at the far end of the bar. Works the docks, mostly. Collects from the unions and shippers both, they say. And they say he skims from Sonny's take but never enough to make Sonny mad. Why?"

I remembered the man at the end of the bar, and stored his face away in my mental files.

"No reason," I said. "You know where he lives?"

"No. Why?"

"No reason. You think you can find out?"

"Probably."

"Let me know, if you find out."

We got into the old Toyota and found a McDonald's.

"Why don't you eat decent food?" complained Quinn, as I worked my way through a Quarter Pounder with cheese, big fries, and a small Coke. "You cook like a dream at home but whenever you get on the mainland you pig out on fast food."

"You don't know how good you've got it," I said. "You can eat like this anytime you

want to, but over on the Blessed Isle we re-
pelled the Big Mac Attack when they tried
to build in Vineyard Haven a while back, so
now we don't have any McDonald's or
Taco Bells, or KFCs, or any place to get decent, cheap, fast, dependable food. So when
I come across the sound to America I eat as
much of this stuff as I can." I waved a fry.
"The whole world can't be wrong, Quinn.
The U.S.A. makes the most popular fast
food on the planet, for God's sake. Wise up.
This is manna from heaven!"

Quinn gave me a sad look.

I took him back to his office building, and
thanked him for his time and his help. "I
hope this doesn't put you in wrong with
Sonny," I said.

"Well, it might not have helped, but it
probably didn't hurt. Sonny never said anything incriminating. I could have taped the
whole thing and I'd still have nothing worth
writing about."

"How about AGGRIEVED HUSBAND CON-
FRONTS GANGSTER IN CHARLESTOWN BAR.
That's a story."

"You want that in the paper?"

"No, no, and no."

"You going to tell me why you want to
know where Pete McBride lives?"

"Sure. So I can track him down if I have

to. I want his address. And his phone number, if you can get it. And find Graham, while you're at it. For the same reason."

"You're something else," said Quinn. He walked into the building and I drove to Jamaica Plain.

The Riminis lived in a big house on a quiet side street. I could see how a couple of schoolteachers might have a hard time paying the mortgage on a place like that.

I parked and went up to the door. The lawn was newly mowed, and there were flowers under the windows and on both sides of the walk. I knocked. The door opened and I was looking into the eyes of the woman I'd loved and married long ago. My heart seemed to hesitate then start again.

"Jeff!"

"Hello, Carla."

"Oh, Jeff, I'm so glad to see you." She put her arms around my neck and pulled my lips down to hers. They were warm, familiar lips and they held mine for a long kiss. Then she put her head on my chest and began to cry.

9

Her body fit against mine as though it was made to be there. Her arms were now around my waist and her soft hair drew my face down so I could inhale the scent of it. My arms were around her and I noticed that my hand was caressing her back. It was a gentle movement, like that I gave to my children when they were sad or hurt.

Abruptly she pulled away and brushed at her eyes. "You must think I'm a complete idiot! Come in." She reached for my hand, then pulled her own back. She turned and I followed her into the house.

She waved me into a chair. "I'll bet you could use a beer!"

"Sure."

"Some things never change." She tried a smile that didn't quite work and went into the kitchen. The beer she brought back was the light kind, but I sipped it anyway. If God wanted us to drink light beer, She'd have made light grain.

Carla sat on the couch. "It's so good to see you again. You haven't changed much in fifteen years." She picked at something imaginary on her sleeve. Her skin looked tight and her eyes were those of a spooked deer.

"A lot of water's gone under the bridge," I said.

"Yes." She leaned forward. "I read about what happened. That PILOT DOWNED AND TRUCKER WRECKED IN ACCIDENT WITH HOUSEWIFE story. It was all my fault! Is your wife going to be all right? I'm so sorry! It was so stupid of me to send Tom there, but I never imagined that those men would come here. . . . I'm such a coward!"

I agreed with some of that, but I said, "Forget it. It's just more of that water. Zee and Diana will be fine. What's important now is that we all get shuck of the guys who are after your husband."

"Where is he? Where's Tom? Is he all right?"

I drank off the rest of my thin-tasting beer and stood up. "Let's go for a walk."

"A walk?" She looked puzzled, but nodded. "All right."

When we went out, there was a blue Lincoln sedan parked about half a block up the street behind my truck. It hadn't been there when I pulled into her driveway. We walked away from the car, up the block, passing other big old houses like hers. It was a nice, quiet street.

"Why are we out here?" she asked.

"Probably for no good reason," I said, "but I want to be careful. There are at least two people who want to find Tom: Sonny Whelen and a guy named Graham, who says he's a cop. I doubt if either one of them has a satellite system to keep track of the people they're interested in, but it's possible that one or both of them have bugged your house or tapped your phone or car. You can go down to your local magazine store and buy a catalog for the stuff you'd need to do that. It's less likely that they have a big ear listening to us out here on the street, so that's why we're here."

She looked around almost wildly. "Do you really think our house might be bugged? I can't believe it. It's like a movie."

"It's not a movie," I said. "It's real life, and your house probably isn't bugged. But if it is, you and Tom can't talk without having somebody else hear every word you say. I think you should play it safe. Do you have any money?"

She looked at me with surprise. "Some. Not much. Our credit cards are used up and I can't pay the bills, but I have a little set aside."

"I think you should buy a couple of cell phones and use them when you and Tom talk. You keep one here and I'll take the other one with me when I leave and get it to him. That way, nobody can trace his calls and find him. Or at least I don't think they can. When you talk you should both be very careful not to say where he is. Don't ask and don't let him tell you. And don't talk for too long, just in case somebody really can trace his location. Keep your messages short and sweet."

"But I want to know where he is! I want to know he's all right."

"And he wants to tell you both things, which is exactly why you have to make sure he doesn't."

"But if the house isn't bugged . . ."

I had to twist the knife a bit. "If you know and the hoods come back, you'll tell again, just like you did last time."

"Oh." She kicked at a small stone on the walk. "Of course I would. I'm such a coward . . ."

I felt a kind of tenderness for her and was glad to cast the knife away. "No. Anyone would tell. The person hasn't been born who can stand up to every torture and threat. Don't be hard on yourself. Just don't ask where Tom is and don't let him tell you. That may give us time to get out of this mess."

Her arm went around mine and she leaned against me. "You don't have to do this, Jeff, but I'm grateful."

Her touch brought back other feelings I thought I'd gotten rid of long ago.

"Don't be grateful yet," I said. "We're still in the stew."

"Why are you doing it at all?" She looked up at me with the soft blue eyes I'd first seen in a college hallway twenty years before and thought I'd since forgotten but hadn't.

Why, indeed? Was it because I'd never really stopped loving her even after I fell in love with Zee? Or because I wanted her to be happier than I had ever made her, because I felt sorry for her and her addicted husband and wanted to save them from his sickness?

I said, "I'm doing it because my family and I are involved and I want to get us uninvolved, and the only way I know how to do that is to get you and Tom uninvolved, too."

"Oh, if only we can do that! This has been a nightmare. You can't imagine. We're schoolteachers, not gangsters. I'm not made for this kind of life."

True, no doubt. She'd not been made for the stresses of being a cop's wife, either. And now she was married to a guy hooked to the mob.

"Your husband has a problem. Problems have solutions."

"Not all of them."

"This one does."

Her arm tightened on mine. "What is it?"

I shook my head. "I don't know yet. But there is one. The thing we have to do is keep Tom out of sight until I've figured it out."

"What will happen to him if they find him?"

I'd given that some thought. "It depends on who does the finding. If it's Sonny, and he thinks Tom will keep his mouth shut and keep bringing in some worthwhile money, Sonny's boys will probably slap him around a little and let him keep slaving for them. If Sonny thinks he'll turn to the cops and talk, they'll do worse. Graham, of course, wants Tom to do just what Sonny doesn't want him to do: be a mole and tell the cops all, then testify in court. If Tom doesn't play ball, Graham will probably arrest him on gambling charges and anything else he thinks might stick. Even if nothing much does, Tom will still be through as a school-teacher and even more broke than he is now. It's a nice pair of pincers he's caught in."

"It's hopeless," she said.

I thought she might be right. "No, it isn't," I said, "but it's best that you know the realities. Now, we should find ourselves a mall or someplace where you can buy a couple of cell phones."

We turned and walked back. The blue sedan was still there. "I see your neighbor owns a Lincoln," I said. "You live in a classy section of town. We didn't have any Lincolns in our part of Somerville when you and I were young."

She glanced at the car, then shook her head. "Somebody's just visiting." Then she smiled. "We had that old Chevy that burned almost as much oil as gas. Remember?"

"I remember." It had been my first car. Twelve years old when I bought it, full of dents and rattles and other needed work that I was too poor to have done. I kept it running by buying motor oil by the case and the cheapest retread tires I could find. Come to think of it, the rusty Toyota Land Cruiser I drove now was even older than the Chevy had been. I hadn't made much progress as far as cars were concerned.

"Go inside and get your purse and your money, and we'll go shopping," I said. "I'll wait for you here."

She squeezed my arm, frowned slightly, and went up the walk and into the house. When the door closed behind her, I went up the street and tapped on the window of the sedan. The man inside showed me an expressionless face. I tapped again and smiled at him. He pushed a button and the window went down. There was another man beyond him, in the passenger seat.

"Whatta you want, buddy?" asked the driver.

"Hello, Pete," I said. "We saw each other in the Green Harp, but we haven't been introduced. I'm J. W. Jackson. Maybe I can simplify your life for you. As soon as Mrs. Rimini collects her purse, she and I are going to the nearest mall or some such place to do some shopping. I'll drive slow enough for you to keep up with us without any problem, but if you get lost, just come back here and wait. We should be home in less than an hour."

"Fuck you," said Pete McBride.

"In case you're wondering what I'm doing here, Mrs. Rimini used to be Mrs. Jackson, as you may know, and even though we've been divorced for fifteen years, I don't want her to be unhappy. You know what I mean, Pete? Now, some of your boss's guys had the mistaken notion that her husband, Tom Rimini, was hiding out at my house down on the Vineyard. They came looking for him there and got themselves shot up some. You probably read about it in the papers. I had a talk with Sonny, and now I've come by to see how Mrs. Rimini was doing, and to assure her that Sonny Whelen won't be bothering her or me anymore. That's right, isn't it, Pete? Sonny doesn't plan on bothering either of us anymore, does he?"

"You got a big mouth. Shut it up."

I tipped my head to one side. "You know something? I just had a thought. I'll bet that Sonny didn't send you here. I'll bet you and your pal over in the suicide seat are here on your own. Am I right, Pete?"

"I'll close his trap," said the man in the passenger seat. He put his hand on the handle of his door.

I let him see me put a hand under my shirt. "It's dangerous to start fights with people you don't know," I said to him. "Look what happened to The Pilot and Howie Trucker. Both of them were twice as tough as you, and I'm at least half as tough as my wife."

"Hold it, Bruno," said McBride. "The dame just came out of the house."

Bruno? I didn't know anybody was ever really named Bruno. I glanced back and saw Carla coming down her sidewalk, looking at me with an inquisitive expression on her face. I turned back to McBride. "I don't know what's up your sleeve, Pete, but I know there's at least one extra ace in any deck you deal. You want to let me know what's on your mind? I'm always willing to listen to a man with new ideas."

"Fuck off," said McBride.

I stood back and pointed a trigger finger at him. "I'll bet you can find me if you want to, Pete. You have a mouth and I have ears, so if you have anything to say to me, I'll listen. Maybe we have some common interests. Meanwhile, I'll tell you what I'll do. I won't tell Sonny that you were here. Is that fair, or what?"

I stepped farther back, the window went up, and I turned and walked to meet Carla. Behind me, I heard the car start and pull away.

"Who was that?" said Carla.

"Just a guy trying to find Chelsea."

"Chelsea? Chelsea's miles from here!"

"Yeah. He was really lost. But I set him straight. Come on, let's go get those phones."

10

When it was time to pay for the phones, though, Carla bit her lip, turned away from the counter, blushing, and looked at the floor. "I'm sorry, Jeff. I can't afford these. I've got a summer job at a shop in the village, and the boys are out mowing lawns right now. But they eat like horses, and I have bills, and our credit cards are all used up."

She was of the class of Americans that equates financial failure with moral failure. I once had been a member of it too, but I had long since abandoned that ethic.

"I know what it's like to be broke," I said. "It can happen to anybody. Jefferson died broke, Rembrandt died broke, van Gogh died broke, and John D. Rockefeller was born and raised broke." I dug out my own seldom-used credit card.

"I can't ask you to . . ."

"Forget it. You need the phones now, and you can pay me back later, when we get this straightened out."

We got two phones and instructions on how to run them, signed up for service, and got out of there. In the truck, I gave one phone to Carla.

"Use this when you talk with Tom. Don't talk in your house or in your car, because cars are just as easy to bug as houses. I'll have Tom use this other one. It won't keep people from being able to listen in, but it will keep them from tracing his calls to a particular place. Your job is to keep him from telling you where he is and from arranging to meet with you. We don't want anybody finding that out."

We drove toward her house.

"This is a terrible way to live," she said. "How long do we have to do this?"

"I don't know." I glanced at her worried face. "I do know this, though: from now on you have to be tough. I think that a lot of what happens from here on out will depend on you, because I don't believe Tom is strong enough to get through this by himself. You have to be the strong one, the smart one."

She shivered, then leaned her head against my shoulder. "I don't want to be strong or smart. I want somebody to hold me."

Everybody knows that feeling. My arm reached around her shoulders and pulled her toward me. "Just till we get to your place," I said.

At her door, she held my hands in hers. Her blue eyes were deep as the sky. "Please come in. The boys won't be home for hours."

I felt like Odysseus hearing the Sirens, and bound myself to the mast. "No. I have to go."

She dropped her eyes. "I'm sorry. Have I offended you?"

"No."

"It's just that I'm afraid and I feel all alone and weak."

Finally, all of us are alone, but I didn't say that. "It's sensible to be afraid," I said, "but you can't let it rule you. Being brave is acting in spite of fear. People who are never afraid are idiots."

She brushed at her eyes. "I wish I were brave, like your Zee, but I'm not."

No one was like Zee. "You're brave enough to see this through," I said. "Here, let me know if you need some more." I gave her most of the cash I had on me.

She looked at the money in her hand. "I can't take this, Jeff!"

I put a finger under her chin and tipped her face up. With my other hand I brushed the tears from her cheeks. "It's just money," I said. "Besides, this is a test."

"I don't understand."

"For years I've been saying that women are more realistic than men. That women live in the real world, but men live in a theoretical one. I've said that men have economic conferences, but women have to buy things every day with real money; that men make speeches about society, but that women actually have the babies, keep the house, and feed the families. You've been doing those things all your life. You're smart and you're strong and you're realistic, so you take this money, because that's what your situation calls for. Some time later, when things work out, you can give it back if you don't need it anymore."

I took my hands away.

She looked up into my eyes for what seemed a long time. Then she said, "All right. Yes, you're right." Her fingers tightened around the bills. "Thank you. I'll pay you back when I can."

She was forlorn but lovely. Her husband was a fool to have imperiled her, and I realized that I was very angry with him for having done it. But then I pushed my anger away, because all of us are fools at one time or another.

"One thing more," I said. "Do you know how I can get in touch with Graham?"

She shook her head. "If Tom knows, he

never told me. I think he's with vice or drug enforcement or something like that, but I'm not sure. Tom would get a call from him and they'd meet someplace, that's all I know. I've never even seen him."

"Tom must have had a way to get in touch with him. Look in his office. Search his desk for a note he might have scribbled. Look in his address book. If you find anything, call me."

"All right."

"And start thinking of your problem as if it were someone else's. Think of how they might resolve it. Don't allow yourself any wishful thinking. Don't be sentimental, be practical."

"I will."

"Good. I'll have Tom call you tonight on this phone. Say, between six and seven, so be out of the house for that hour."

"Yes. Jeff . . ."

"Yes?"

"Will you kiss me?"

Of course I would.

Her lips were soft and hungry. Finally, I pulled away. She smiled and shook her head. "Sorry. I need a man, I guess."

"I almost wish I were him, but I'm not. We'll get yours back to you before too long."

"The sooner the better," said Carla. "I'm

definitely not the nun type." She touched her tongue to her lips. "I don't suppose you want to come in and check out Tom's office for yourself?"

"Too dangerous," I said, feeling a crooked smile on my face. I turned and walked to the Land Cruiser. She was still on the porch, looking toward me, when I drove away.

I couldn't understand how I'd ever left her. Then I remembered that she had left me.

I hadn't been a member of the Boston PD for fifteen years, but I still knew some guys on the force, so I drove back into Boston, put the Land Cruiser in a parking garage because street parking in Boston is almost impossible, and walked into what I hoped was the right precinct station. Like most of the older inner-city stations it was dingy and smelled of air freshener, soap, dirt, body emissions, and other unidentifiable odors. At the desk I gave my name and asked for Detective Gordon R. Sullivan.

Sullivan was at his desk. He put out his big hand and I took it.

"J. W. Jackson. It's been a while. How's your beautiful wife? Am I right in believing she's the one I've been reading about in the local scandal sheets?"

"She's the one. She's got a bullet crease

across some ribs and a lot of bruises, but she'll be fine."

"Sonny Whelen's lost several people lately. First Ralph Shepard and now these two."

"Who's Ralph Shepard?"

"Past tense. Who *was* Ralph Shepard? Shepard was Sonny's drug wholesaler in Jamaica Plain. Got himself blown away a while back. Probably by the guy who took over the business."

"And who is that?"

"I wish I knew, and so does Sonny. Whoever it is, is the community distributor now. Sonny would like to get the territory back, but so far no luck."

"Too bad."

"Yeah. I won't miss having The Pilot and Trucker around. The stories in the papers anywhere near accurate?"

"Pretty much." I told him what I knew about what had happened at my house.

He nodded. "Well, usually I don't think much of civilians having handguns in the house, but this time I'm glad she had one. I wonder what Sonny Whelen thinks about having two of his hired apes put down for the count by a lone woman."

"I can tell you something about that," I said, and related the tale of my meeting with

Sonny in the Green Harp.

"Well, well," said Sullivan. "Someday you may look back on that and call yourself lucky that nobody just shot you on the spot, carried your carcass out through the kitchen, and dumped it off a bridge later. Over in parts of Charlestown people are blind when stuff like that happens. They never see a thing."

"There's more," I said, and told him of meeting Tom Rimini and Carla and what they'd told me about their problems. I told him everything I knew or thought I knew about Rimini, except where he was. I don't tell anybody everything. "I'm trying to get ahold of this cop Graham," I said. "If I can get Rimini and his family out from under, I want to do it. Maybe Graham can help."

"Where's Rimini now?"

"He left my place yesterday morning. I haven't seen him since."

Sullivan put a stick of gum in his mouth and chewed it while he looked at me. "Naturally you don't know where he went."

"Naturally not."

"How come you're going out of your way to give him a hand?"

"I'm not always too sure."

He chewed. "The wife, maybe?"

"Not the way you think. Just call me senti-mental."

"Sentimental you." He chewed some more, then shrugged. "What do you want from me?"

"I want to talk to Graham. I was hoping you could put me in touch."

"I don't know him, but I'll ask around. Do you know if he's local, state, or fed?"

"No. I don't think Rimini knows, either."

"Hmmph. You know, I hate these new no-smoking rules. I'm wearing out my jaw chewing gum! I'll ask around and let you know. Gimme your number. I think I have it around somewhere, but I don't know where, so give it to me again."

I did that, then pointed at his phone.

"Go ahead," said Sullivan.

I called Quinn. He wasn't at his desk. I tried his apartment. He wasn't there either. I thanked Sullivan and went out.

At the parking lot I got the Land Cruiser, paid the ransom they wanted for keeping it safe from the meter maids, and got out of Boston just ahead of the evening traffic jam.

I was lucky to have gotten myself a return reservation because new summer people were already lined up to catch the ferry out to Eden. I stood on the top deck and watched the cars and walkers come aboard.

Where did all these people come from? Where did they live? What did they do for a living? Were any of them from Charlestown? Did any of them work for Sonny Whelen or Pete McBride? Was one of them named Graham?

The boat's whistle blew and we pulled out into the sound. I went to the foredeck and watched the low outline of the Vineyard grow larger. There were sailboats heading into Woods Hole and others reaching for island harbors. The waves were fair-sized and the boats were leaning and casting a lot of spray, so the crews were in foul weather gear. Up there on the ferry's deck I was high above the water. I was glad to be leaving the mainland behind, although I knew I wasn't leaving my troubles there.

11

Zee met me at the door. She winced when I forgot and hugged her too hard.

"Sorry."

"That's okay." Our kiss was gentle because of her split lip. She ran her hands through my hair and looked up at me. "I've been fending off reporters all day. Come and have a drink with me and tell me what you've been up to."

The vodka was in the freezer and the olives, green for me and black for Zee, were in the fridge, and so I made quick work of building our vermouthless martinis and carrying them up to the balcony. There, while the kids played in the yard below, I told her about everything except the kisses.

"And how was Carla?" asked my wife, looking out over the pond at the boats in the sound beyond the barrier beach.

"Broke, worried, and wondering what to do."

"And you're going to save her and her husband."

"I'm trying to save us, mostly. I don't want any more thugs in our lives."

"It seems like you've accomplished that. Sonny Whelen says he made a mistake."

"Yeah. Except for one little thing. I told Sonny that I didn't know where Tom Rimini is, but I do. If Sonny finds out, he might not be happy."

She stared off to the east for a long minute, then said, "I don't like any of this. I think you should tell Tom Rimini to get off the island and go somewhere else, and then you should tell Sonny Whelen that he's gone."

The idea made sense, but even as I agreed that it did, I thought of Carla's fears and saw her soft, troubled face.

"I'll talk with Rimini," I said. "I'll give him the cell phone and tell him what happened up in Boston. There may be a way to get him out of this and get him and his family back into a decent life."

"It's because of her, isn't it?" said Zee, with that insight that baffles men. "That's why you're doing it."

There was no escaping the truth of her suspicions. "Yes. I think so, at least. I'd probably be handling this some other way if it wasn't for her."

Her voice was tight, and her hand strayed to her bruised jaw. "If it wasn't for her, none of this would have happened."

She wasn't only thinking of her own hurts, she was thinking of the man she had killed and the man she had mutilated, and of possible troubles to come.

"I know," I said. "I wish it never had, but it did. And now it has to be dealt with."

"You don't owe her anything."

I had been thinking about that. "Maybe not," I said, "but if I don't help her and things get worse than they already are, I know I'll always wish I'd tried."

"You're married to me now!"

I was surprised by the emotion in her voice, and tried to keep my own gentle and soothing. "You and the kids are the most important things in my life, but I'd like to think that if what's happened to Carla had happened to any other woman, to some woman I didn't even know, that I'd try to help her, too."

"You're not Galahad. You should let the police handle it. Let that man Graham take care of it."

"I'm trying to get in touch with him."

She emptied her glass and stared down at it. "Do you still love her?"

I said nothing.

She took a deep breath.

"I don't know if love's the word," I said. "I know I loved her once a long time ago. I know I kept on loving her for a long time after she left me, but then that love finally faded into something else. Today I found out that I'm still attracted to her and still care about her and want her to be happy and that I think her husband is a fool to have endangered her the way he has. But I don't love her the way I love you; the way a man loves the only real woman in his life."

I watched her as she plucked the two black olives from her glass and ate them. Then she got up and went down the stairs.

I felt a great coldness inside my soul. The world was suddenly without form and void, and as I stared out at Nantucket Sound, there was darkness upon the face of the deep.

Time must have passed; then I heard her step on the stairs and she was there again. She kissed me and took my hand. "And I love you, too," she said. "The way a woman loves the only real man in her life."

And it was evening of the very first day.

Something was in my eye. I brushed it away.

"Pa!"

I looked down at Joshua. "What?"

"Can we come up?"

How could I say no? "No," I said. "This is

big-people time. We'll be down soon."

"Pa?"

"What?"

"Can't we have a dog?"

"No! No dogs! We have cats at this house."

"A dog might be nice," said Zee.

Three against one, but I stood firm. "No dogs," I said. "You have to take them for walks, you have to clean up their shit, and they're like damned slaves: they always want to know what you want them to do. They slobber and wag their tails and pant and say what do you want me to do? What do you want me to do? Tell me and I'll do it! Pant, pant, slobber, slobber, wag, wag. I don't like slaves. Give me cats every time. Cats don't give a damn what you want; they only want what they want."

"You're given to long speeches today," said Zee.

"No dogs. Period."

"Ma!"

"What?"

"Can we come up, now?"

"No."

"Can we have a dog?"

"Your father says no."

Oliver Underfoot and Velcro sat beside the catnip in the garden and looked up at us.

They didn't want a dog either; that was obvious. That made it three to three, not three to one. I wasn't in a minority after all.

The evening sunlight cast our shadows on the lawn. My glass was empty. I ate my olives. I wished Tom Rimini had never gambled his first dollar. I looked at my watch.

"I'll give Rimini a call to let him know I'm coming over. I'll be back in time to make supper."

"I took the liberty of rinsing and bagging the clams you got yesterday. They're in the fridge, waiting for you to decide what to do with them."

"Thanks. I had in mind eating them."

"A good plan, but right now I've got bluefish and veggies marinating. All you have to do is slap them on the grill."

"Bachelors are idiots."

"You won't get any argument from me, McGee."

We went downstairs and were met by the little ones.

"Can we go up, Pa? Can we go up, Ma?"

"Oh, dear," said Zee.

"Be careful," I said. "If you fall, you'll break your necks!"

"Just for a little while, then," said Zee. "And no climbing on the railing! Joshua, you make sure that Diana doesn't climb on it, and don't you climb on it either! Diana, don't climb on the railing! Do you understand me?"

"Yes, Ma."

They galloped up the stairs, with Zee's frown following them.

"I think I'll stay out in the yard and keep an eye on them."

I, too, had learned that being a parent meant being worried about your children a lot of the time. You couldn't stop worrying, but at the same time you had to let them go, you had to let them grow away from your arms.

"Okay," I said. "I'll call Rimini."

But when I dialed John Skye's number I got a busy signal.

It was more than irksome, it was dangerous. One traced call and Rimini's safe haven was no longer that.

I hung up, waited, and dialed again. Still a busy signal.

I went out into the yard where Zee, eyes shaded by one hand as she looked up into the setting sun, was watching her children enjoy their rare visit to the balcony.

"I'll be back," I said, and drove away.

John Skye had bought his old farm years before when prices were a lot lower than they had been since. Zee and I had been married in his yard, between the house and the barn, and I knew the place well, since I opened it in the spring, closed it up in the fall, and kept an eye on it during the winter. My favorite room was his library, which was filled with books most of which I had never read. It had seemed the perfect place to hide Tom Rimini, but no place is perfect for people who won't stay hidden.

Rimini's green Honda was in the yard when I pulled in. The barn would have been a better place for it, but Rimini apparently hadn't thought of that.

I knocked on the door and when Rimini opened it even I could hear the anger in my voice: "I thought we had a deal. You agreed to make your calls from somewhere else! Every time you make a call from here you take a chance on having it traced!"

He backed away, his eyes worried and wary. "What . . . what do you mean? I haven't called anybody."

"I just tried to phone you. The line was busy. Twice!"

"What? When?"

"Just now. Ten minutes ago!"

"Oh. Oh, that wasn't me calling out. That was someone calling your friend John Skye. I told them he was in Colorado."

"It took you quite a while to tell them

that. I tried to get through to you twice."

He licked his upper lip. "Sorry. We chatted a few minutes. You know . . ."

"Who was it?"

"Oh, gosh. I . . . I don't remember. He said he'd get in touch with your friend later in the summer."

"And who did you say you were?"

"I said I was doing some work on the plumbing. It was the first thing I could think of. I figured old places like this always have problems with plumbing."

I felt the anger ease out of me. I gave him the cell phone and told him to use it when he called Carla between six and seven. "She'll be out of the house and waiting for your call."

"Why should she be out of the house?"

"In case the place has been bugged."

His eyes widened. "Bugged?"

"Yeah. Your car, too. We should have it checked out. It may have a homing device of some kind on it, too, come to think of it."

"I don't know how to do that! And who . . . ?" He paused. "You mean . . . ?" A worried look appeared on his face. I thought it was overdue.

"That's right," I said. "There are several possibilities. Whelen and Graham are two of them. Pete McBride might be another. I know a guy who can check out your car. He's an old hand at such stuff. I'll see him tomorrow."

Rimini eyed me uneasily. "Pete McBride? You know about him?"

"I know he's another player. I just don't know his game. Let's sit down."

We sat at the kitchen table and I told him about my day in Boston. I didn't tell him about my feelings for his wife or the kisses we'd exchanged, but I told him the rest. He listened without comment. When I was through, he was chewing on his lower lip.

"What can I do? I don't want anything to happen to Carla and the boys." He darted a glance at me. "You say you think that Pete McBride wants Sonny's job. What if he gets it? Will that get me off this hook? I owe Sonny money, but I don't owe any to Pete McBride."

I was pretty sure that in the unlikely event Pete managed to depose King Sonny, he would no doubt lay claim to any money owed to Sonny, but I saw no point in troubling Rimini with that thought. A false hope was, for the moment, probably better than no hope at all.

"I want to get in touch with Graham," I said. "How do I do it?"

He rubbed his hands together as I'd seen

him do before. "I don't know."

I didn't believe him. "You must know. You had to be able to get in touch with him."

"No. Really. He always got in touch with me. He'd call and we'd meet someplace. In a café or a bar. Never the same place twice in a row."

I stared at him, sure he was lying, but not knowing why he was doing it. His eyes shifted away, then came back. His hands rubbed some more.

"I'm telling you the truth," he said. "I wouldn't lie to you. Why should I?"

I couldn't guess. I got up. "Use the cell phone to call your wife between six and seven, but don't use this phone for any reason. I'll be back tomorrow and we'll check out your car for bugs."

I drove home full of doubts and questions.

12

Joe Begay, who grew up near Oraibi, out in Arizona, and claimed to be of mostly Navajo and Hopi blood, had been my sergeant in the long ago Asian war in which I'd participated so briefly at age seventeen, when I still thought combat might be an adventure. By the time I'd been released from the VA hospital weeks later, he was out of my life and had not come into it again until he married a Vineyard girl who happened to be a friend of Zee's. Toni, his wife, was one of the Vanderbecks who lived up in what was then Gay Head but is now officially Aquinnah, hometown for most of the island's Wampanoags. Their daughter, Hanna, had been unofficially engaged to Joshua since both were babes in arms. Hanna was an older women, having emerged into the outer world two weeks earlier than Josh, but both Zee and Toni agreed that it was good for a woman to have a younger man, so she could raise him the way she wanted him to be.

Joe was supposedly retired from whatever never-explained international work he had been doing for the previous quarter of a century, but still occasionally went away some-where for short periods of time to deal with business affairs he never described and about which I never asked; which was, per-haps, one of the reasons we had become friends.

He was a big V-shaped guy with wide shoulders, a thick chest, and narrow hips, and was, in my opinion, the second most dangerous man on Martha's Vineyard, the first being Cousin Henry Bayles, who lived in retirement in Oak Bluffs and who was old enough to be Joe's father and half his size. Cousin Henry's edge was that he looked frail and elderly, but was a onetime Phila-delphia gangster who knew how to kill you in a variety of ways, and who was totally without fear of death. I liked them both, al-though I did not socialize with Cousin Henry as I did with Joe and Toni Begay.

When I needed certain technical assis-tance or information having to do with gov-ernment activities, I went to Joe, who, if he didn't already have the information on hand, could generally find out what I needed to know. In spite of being retired, he had both a lockjaw memory and endless contacts.

Since the Jacksons en masse hadn't seen the Begays lately, and since normally bright and shiny Zee was in a somber, postshooting mood and, I thought, probably in need of some woman talk, I prevailed upon her to come with me the next morning. She smiled, and we all got into her little Jeep, and drove to John Skye's house, where Tom Rimini uneasily gave up his car and promised to stay put until I brought it back. Then I followed Zee and the sprats up to Aquinnah, the Vineyard's westernmost town.

Usually, in the United States, probably because of the historic march of the European conquerors of the land, citizens go up North, down South, out West, and back East; but on Martha's Vineyard we go up West and down East. The most popular explanation for this, and for going down to Maine and up from there to Boston, is that the prevailing southwest winds usually obliged sailing ships to beat upwind when going to the west and vice versa. This day we didn't sail to Aquinnah but we went up there anyhow.

Aquinnah, famed for its cliffs of colored clay, is one of the Vineyard's best places for fishing, particularly for bass. It's a lovely, hilly, windswept place, offering fine views of the Elizabeth Islands and Noman's Land, but was and is my least favorite town on the island because of its politics: its roads are lined with no-parking, no-stopping, and no-pausing signs that keep fishermen from its beaches, and its parking lot charges its victims a fortune and a half. Worse yet, while it caters to buses full of often elderly tourists with equally elderly bowels and bladders, it offers only pay toilets to its visitors, a practice that is clearly an abomination in the eyes of man and God.

Fortunately for me, I have friends there who have yards to park in and toilets they let me use for free. Joe and Toni Begay are two of them. The Begays live in a neat house not far from the beach north of the cliffs, and it was there that our small caravan parked and unloaded.

Toni, new babe on her hip and Hanna by her side, greeted us with kisses. Joe limited his kisses to Zee, and then held her and looked down at her battered face.

"How are you doing?" he asked.

"I'm okay. I think."

He nodded. "It takes time to get over the kind of trouble you've had. Now, tell me, did you come up here to talk with me, or to visit with my wife?"

She managed a smile. "Do I have to choose?"

He was not quite old enough to be her father, but he acted the part. "Go talk with Toni. She gets tired of wasting her voice on my ears."

"I do not," said Toni. "But come on, Zee. Let's leave these guys alone so they can bond."

"I don't know if we want to bond," said Begay.

"Try. Come on, Zee. I'll pour us some coffee and we can discuss Hanna and Joshua's marriage."

The women and children went into the house. Begay's eyes followed them. "How's she really doing?"

I didn't know, but I said what I believed. "Her brain knows she did what she had to do, but it goes against her training and her feelings about how people should live. She's a nurse, and nurses cure, they don't kill."

"You any help to her?"

"I don't think so, but I plan to keep on trying."

He nodded. "Do that, and she'll probably be okay. People fight wars and see and do terrible things, but then come home again and mostly are just fine, normal folks afterward."

"I know. But some don't get over it. I don't want her to be one of those. Especially since she did the right thing."

"Maybe Toni will be some help." He tipped his head to one side. "You just come up here into Indian country so our wives can chat, or did you have something else in mind?"

"Well, as a matter of fact . . ." I gave him the short version of Tom Rimini's troubles and my concerns about his car.

"In this country, bugging cars and phones is usually government work," said Begay. "The most the bad guys manage, generally, is listening in on police radio calls and stuff like that, so while they're robbing the liquor store or knocking off an armored car, they'll know where the cops are. But let's have a look."

I watched as he looked under the hood, inside the passenger area, in the trunk, and finally, under the car.

"Well," he said, standing and dusting himself off. "Unless somebody took an awful lot of time to hide his work and used some gimmick I never heard of, I'd say your Mr. Rimini owns an unbugged car."

"Good. That's one thing I don't have to worry about, then."

"Why are you worried at all?"

"His wife was my wife."

Begay's craggy face could be as expressionless as stone. "Ah," he said. Then, "But she isn't anymore."

"I know. It's difficult to explain."

"Not so difficult," said Begay. "Old loyalties die hard."

A troublesome truth.

"While I've got you in my clutches," I said, "there's something else. I have a couple of other people working on this, but one more won't hurt. In your travels did you ever meet a cop named Graham?"

"Now that's some question. I've met a lot of people in my life. Can you narrow it down?"

"A guy with a badge. I don't have a first name. He's got his hooks in Rimini. According to Rimini, Graham wants him to rat on Sonny Whelen. Rimini's wife, Carla, didn't know much about him, but told me she thought he was in vice or narcotics. Quinn — you know him? — reporter for *The Globe*?"

"You take him fishing sometimes."

"That's the guy. I've got him looking for Graham and I've asked a cop I know in Boston to look, too. So far, no luck. Now I'm asking you."

Begay stared into space. I wondered why we do that when we're thinking, or why we put hands to our chins or foreheads or rub our skulls.

"RICO," said Begay. "If Graham's a fed,

he's probably trying to nail Whelen for rack-eteering. He isn't really interested in your friend Rimini at all. He just wants to use him to get at Whelen."

"That's how I figure it, but . . ."

"But what?"

"Carla thought he might be in vice, which would make sense if he's interested in gambling and small-time bookies like Rimini, but she also thought he might be a narc."

"She's a schoolteacher. She probably doesn't know a narc from a nasturtium. It's just a word she's heard people use."

"Probably, but maybe not. What if he is a narc? What does that mean?"

"It means that your pal Rimini may be up to more hanky-panky than taking bets from schoolkids."

I tried to picture it: Tom Rimini, drug dealer. All things are possible, of course, but I actually had trouble seeing Rimini as a bookie, let alone a dealer. "He's not my pal," I said.

"I'll tell you what," said Begay. "I'll make some calls and see if I can get a handle on this guy Graham. If he's in Justice and is working around Boston for the Criminal Division or the DEA or whatever, I might be able to track him down. What do you want with him?"

"I want to talk with him. I want to see if there's a way out of this mess for Rimini and his family."

"Like what?"

"Witness protection, maybe. Something like that."

Begay dug into a shirt pocket and came out with tobacco and papers. He rolled a neat cigarette and lit it. I could roll a cigarette just like that, even though I'd long since given up smoking. I'd learned the art during my youthful marijuana days. Cigarette rolling is like bicycle riding; once you know how, you never forget. I sniffed Begay's exhalation. Prince Albert, for sure. Crimp cut, for a good roll. I missed my pipe. Do we ever get over our addictions?

Was Carla one of mine?

"Don't treat Zee like she was made of glass," said Begay, catching me quite off guard. "Treat her the way you would normally. I don't think that tiptoeing around hurt people is good for them. I think we should treat them the way we treat anybody else." He finished the cigarette and ground the butt into the dirt with his shoe. "Bad habit, but I can't quite shake it. Come on. Let's go join the ladies."

We went into the house and found the engaged couple, their mothers, and their younger siblings enjoying food and drink.

"I'm glad to see that you manly men have completed your business and are ready to rejoin society," said Toni. "Would you like some milk and cookies?"

"Cookie, yes; milk, no," said Begay.

I agreed. Chocolate chips are good anytime of day or night. We tested them. Up to snuff.

"We're just about to take a walk along the beach," said Zee. "We invite you to join us."

Begay and I exchanged glances. "We accept," I said, and Begay took the baby from his wife's arms.

A path led from the house west to the beach, where the summer wind was slapping waves against the shore. Hanna and Joshua and Diana played tag with the water while the rest of us watched and strolled. It was a lovely morning, and my troubles seemed far, far away. But then I looked out across the gentle blue waters toward the Devil's Bridge where, on January 18, 1884, at three forty-five in the morning, the *City of Columbus* had struck the rocks and 121 lives had been lost, many of the bodies washed, frozen, onto this very beach. There is no away. I took Zee's hand and held it.

13

Long ago, when I was in a hospital having Viet Cong shrapnel taken out of my legs, I had the opportunity to get past some of my earlier illusions and reduce life to its fundamentals. In my case they were, as far as I could determine, the need for work — it made no difference what kind as long as it brought me simple food; the need for shelter — any kind that would protect me from the elements; the need for a woman — because I was inescapably heterosexual; and the need for a male friend — because there are some human experiences that only people of the same gender can understand. Nothing else was really important; not wealth, not honors, not acclaim, not power, not a big house, not a fine car, not a prestigious profession, not dozens of friends; none of these. They were all only indulgences, fripperies, adornments — to be enjoyed but not to be taken seriously.

Over two decades later, I hadn't changed my mind about those fundamentals. I might be the man in Zee's life, but I knew she needed more than I could offer, so I was pleased that Toni was her friend. I thought

Zee was looking better, more thoughtful and less moody, by the time we said our good-byes and headed back down-island, and I credited Toni for that.

Zee and the tots drove home, and I drove Rimini's car to John Skye's house. Rimini didn't open the door of the house until I stepped out of the car and he could see from the window who I was.

I gave him the keys. "Your car is clean," I said. "No bugs."

"Oh, good." Rimini seemed relieved, as well he should be.

"It's one less thing to worry about. Now, I'm trying to track down your friend Graham. If I can get in touch with him, we may be able to find a way for you to get out from under Whelen's thumb."

The mention of Graham's name changed the expression on Rimini's face. It became furtive, like that of a cat caught eyeing the goldfish bowl.

"Graham? How can you find Graham? Why do you need to find him?"

His look perplexed me. "I know Graham hassled you," I said, "but Sonny Whelen is the one who sent two enforcers after you, so if you have to choose between Graham and Sonny, you'll be smart to go for Graham. You saw his badge. He may wave jail in your face to get you to work with him, but he's not going to shoot off your kneecaps."

He rubbed those hands of his. "I don't think you should try to deal with Graham. I don't trust him. I don't know what to do, but I don't think Graham can help me. You should leave him out of this. I don't want to go to jail."

I studied him, wondering what was going on in his head, wondering what he wasn't telling me, wishing that he would be straight with me but doubting that he ever would, feeling sorry for Carla for having married him, but immediately backing off from that because I couldn't know what drew them together, what they saw or needed in each other.

"Look," I said, "you may not trust Graham, but he's a player whether you like him or not. If you want me to try to help get you off this hook you're on, let me do it my way. If you don't, it's fine with me; you're on your own. You can leave right now."

He collected himself. "I just need time to let things work out. While they do, I need to be someplace where Sonny can't find me for a few days. You've done enough for me already, and I thank you for it, but if I can just stay here for a while, things will be fine. I know they will."

Such naïveté was irritating and almost incomprehensible to me. "Sonny Whelen isn't the forgive-and-forget type," I said. "He's the kind who remembers."

Rimini made sweeping gestures with his hands as I imagined he did when he was persuading his students to accept some notion alien to them. "Trust me, J.W. I know things are going to be all right. You go on home to your family. They need you. Just let me stay here alone for a few days. I'll get some groceries and I'll use the cell phone to talk with Carla, and everything will get worked out."

I was tired of him, but still tied to him by the lie I'd told Whelen. "Give me a ride home," I said.

"Of course, of course. I hope you're not angry."

I tried not to be. "Anger is a useless emotion. I try to avoid it."

He dropped me off in front of our house.

"Thanks," I said. "If you need anything, give me a call. I'll check on you later."

"Please telephone me before you come," he said. "It spooks me when a car comes into the yard. Even yours."

Timorous Tom. Still, I couldn't quite blame him for being nervous. For the immediate future, I expected to be wary of cars coming down my own driveway. It was not the way I wanted to live. I watched him drive away, then went into the house.

Zee and the children were eating lunch. Bluefish salad. Yum. I joined them.

"A woman wants me to be on the *Today* show," said Zee. "I said no."

"Good."

Afterward, we all went out to the garden, where Josh and Diana helped their mother and me do some weeding, with the big people instructing the little people about the difference between the little green plants we wanted to keep and those we didn't. Such choices were not always easily made, but since it was only June we could replant most of the erroneously plucked veggies. Gardening was a Vineyard activity much more to my liking than my morning's efforts. It was good to work shoulder to shoulder with Zee, getting dirt under our nails while the summer sun beat down on our backs, and it was good to wash up together afterward.

"If we can find a painter," said Zee, reaching for a towel, "maybe we could pose for a *Modern American Gothic*. You can hold a hoe instead of a pitchfork, and I'll borrow some reading specs."

"We can do seasonal *Gothics*, with Vivaldi scores sneaked into the background where

144

you really have to look hard to see them. We can do summer with a hoe, fall with a scallop net, winter with a quahog rake, and spring with a shovel."

"We'll be famous all year round. We can make prints and get rich."

"Fame and wealth at last."

"Does this mean I can have a bathroom of my own?"

"Do you want a bathroom of your own?"

"Every woman wants a bathroom of her own."

"I didn't know."

"There's a lot you don't know about women, your hunkiness."

My hunkiness. That sounded good, even though it was an ignorant sort of hunkiness. Still, ignorant hunkiness was better than no hunkiness at all.

"My hunkiness is your hunkiness," I said, leering down at her.

Her arms came up around my neck. "I'm glad."

Joshua's voice entered my consciousness.

"Pa, when you finish kissing Ma will you play ball?"

I held Zee gently against me.

"Pa? Will you?"

"I want to play, too," said Diana's voice. "It's not fair if I don't get to play!"

"See what fertility gets you?" I whispered in Zee's ear. "This is all your doing."

"Not quite mine alone," said Zee, dropping a hand below my belly and gripping. "This had something to do with it."

"Oh my, I guess you're right," I said in my best falsetto.

We went to play with our children. Life seemed simple and good and as it ought to be. But not for long. The phone rang, and I went in to answer it.

It was the Chief, calling from the courthouse. "There's an assistant D.A. here. He wants to talk with your wife about what happened. How's she feeling? If she's not up to it, maybe I can hold him off awhile."

I glanced out into the yard and saw that Zee was laughing.

"I'll ask her. She already made her statement, didn't she?"

"He wants to talk with her himself. You know how it goes. Whenever there's a homicide, there's the possibility of a trial. D.A.'s thrive on being crime fighters, and this is a pretty high-profile case. Housewife outshoots big-city gunmen and all that. He's got some questions and sooner or later she'll have to talk with him. You got a lawyer?"

"The only lawyer I know lives up in Boston. Why? Does she need a lawyer?"

"Everybody needs a lawyer one time or another."

It's an age of litigation. "Wait," I said. I went out and told Zee about the call. "What do you want to do?" I asked.

Her bruised face had lost its laughter. "I'll talk with the Chief."

She went in and I tossed the ball between Josh and Diana, neither of whom was quite ready to try out for the Red Sox. After a while, Zee came outside, carrying her purse.

"I'll go down. I don't have anything to hide, and I want to get this past me."

"Even people with nothing to hide need lawyers. Maybe I should call Brady Coyne."

"Brady is in Boston. The D.A. is right here in Edgartown."

I was an American and therefore by definition leery of people in authority. "I think I'll call him anyway. Maybe he knows somebody down here who can go with you."

"I don't need anybody to go with me," said Zee. "You stay here with the kids and I'll be back pretty soon."

"I'm going with you."

"No, you're not! I don't need tending!" Her voice was sharp. She walked to her little Jeep, got in without another glance at me, and drove away.

"Pa, throw the ball!"

I tossed it toward Diana. "You two play together for a while."

I went inside and phoned Brady Coyne's office. Julie, his receptionist/secretary/factotum, answered. I had never met Julie, but I knew her voice well. Her voice said that Mr. Coyne was out.

"With or without his fly rod?"

"He's never without his fly rod, Mr. Jackson. You should know that."

"Call me J.W. Yeah, it was a dumb question."

"What can Mr. Coyne do for you, Mr. Jackson?"

"You hear the girl-guns-goons story?"

"Everybody's heard it. The NRA and I are in agreement about this one, for a change. How's your wife doing?"

"That's why I'm calling." I told her about the assistant D.A.

"She should have waited," said Julie. "Mr. Coyne visited a client in Amherst this morning, but he had me reschedule a couple of appointments he had this afternoon. There are a lot of trout streams out west of Boston, so there's no telling when he'll be back. The man has no sense of business at all. He's lucky that he's smart and has me to give him reality checks from time to time. I'll leave your message and tell him to call you when he gets in. Your wife probably did as well without a lawyer as she would have with one, so don't worry."

But I did worry. And I worried some more when Zee finally got home, because she looked tired and irritated.

"How'd it go?"

"I didn't like him," she said. "He reminded me of a snake."

Another serpent in Eden.

"How about a drink? It's almost cocktail time."

"Make mine a double."

I made two doubles.

14

A reporter from a women's magazine called during supper and was thanked for the call and told that we'd be giving no interviews. She hoped I'd change my mind. I said I didn't think we would. Brady Coyne called about seven-thirty. I told him about the meeting between Zee and the snake.

"Well," said Brady, "being a lawyer myself, I naturally think that people should never talk with D.A.'s or cops or anybody else without having their own lawyers right there, but most of us do it anyway, even lawyers who should know better. Let me talk with Zee."

I handed Zee the phone and went back to trying to teach Joshua and Diana how to play chess. After a while, needing R and R, we changed to Crazy Eights. At the outer edge of my hearing zone, Zee seemed to be doing more listening than talking. When she hung up, she came and watched the game until it was bedtime for the tads. After we'd read to them and gotten them cozy under their blankets, we sat beside each other on the living room couch. I put my arm around her shoulders. She leaned against me.

"Brady says a lot of assistant D.A.'s look like snakes and that this case had gotten a lot of publicity so the D.A., being a political creature, is definitely going to see if he can get some brownie points from it for himself. He asked me what the snake said and what I said and told me not to talk with anybody again unless I have a lawyer with me. He said he'd get in touch with an island lawyer and have him contact me. He said he'd contact the D.A. and let him know that he and my island lawyer were representing me from now on. He said he was pretty sure that the D.A. will eventually call a press conference to announce that he's not bringing any charges, but that you never really know, so I should just keep my mouth shut and give no interviews and go on with my life. I told him I would."

"Good."

"He said his fee would be our guest room during the derby this fall and a fishing partner to show him the hot spots."

"Good again. The price is right."

"But I don't know if I can really just get on with my life. I wonder if I'll ever get over this."

I thought of the men and women who come home from war and get right back to regular living in spite of what they'd seen and done. It's always amazed me that almost all of them are completely normal people living completely normal lives.

"You probably won't get totally over it, but you will get on with your life. It'll take a while."

She took my hand in hers and pulled my arm tighter around her as if she were cold in spite of the warm summer night. "You still have that bad war dream sometimes, even after all these years."

I knew which dream she meant. It was the dream of the mortar attack on my platoon. In it I again heard the tremendous sounds and felt the shocks and saw the bushes and trees exploding and saw the blood, and the dream would blow me, terrorized, out of sleep, cold and sweaty, not knowing if I was really shouting or just imagining that I was.

"It doesn't happen very often anymore," I said. "Living with you has kept it away. If you have any dreams about this business, I want to keep them away from you."

"I'm a nurse, so I'm used to the results of violence. What I'm not used to is being the violent one. It makes me sick to think that I killed that man and would have killed the other one without a thought."

"You didn't do it without a thought. You

did it because you could still think clearly in spite of being hammered by a man twice your size. If you hadn't killed Logan and shot Trucker, they'd have killed you and Diana too. I'll always be in your debt for what you did. You saved my wife and daughter."

She squeezed my hand. "My head tells me that, but some other part of me feels sick."

"That's your goodness. If you didn't feel sick, you'd be just like Logan. Logan never felt sick about any violent thing he ever did. He killed people and maimed people and probably raped women and never lost a minute of sleep over it. You're not like Logan or Trucker or Sonny Whelen or any of their kind."

She moved restlessly. "How long did it take you to get over shooting that thief in Boston, when you were a policeman?"

"It took a while," I said. "It's gotten pretty distant, but I really don't want to forget it, because you shouldn't forget a thing like that."

"I think that, too, because what's happened to me is like what happened to you. She shot you first, and she'd have killed you if you hadn't killed her."

"She tried pretty hard, and I'd do what I did again, but it's a hell of a thing. Like Clint said in that movie, I took everything she had and everything she ever would have."

"Yes." She was quiet for a while. Then she said, "Here we are. Mr. and Mrs. Killer Jackson."

I looked down at her face. She wasn't crying, she was just staring at the fireplace.

"No, you're no killer. You're a good woman who had to kill a very bad man. Logan and Trucker and Whelen are the killers in this story. You saved Diana and yourself the only way you could."

I was saying the same thing over and over, because it was all I could think of to say. I held Zee against me until it was time for bed. There I held her some more until, at last, she drifted into uneasy sleep.

The next morning, as I fed a mushroom and onion omelette to the starving cubs, Zee came out of the bedroom wearing her white uniform.

"I'm going in to work. I've been out most of the week. It's time to rejoin the world. I called in, and they need me."

She'd used her makeup well, but Logan's blows were still evident in that split lip, the swelling of her jaw, and the dark bruise around one eye.

I nodded and pointed at her chair. "Good, but eat first."

"I'll grab something at work."

She kissed the kids and me, and left.

I wondered how the people she worked with would treat her. I figured that she wondered the same thing. Would she be heroine or pariah or neither? I hoped they'd just be glad to have her back. I was pleased, in any case, that she was going to work. I took it to mean that she was trying to put the shooting where it belonged: in that half-forgotten file where we store our misfortunes and our self-doubts so we can get on with our lives.

The phone rang. I answered, listened, said thanks for the call but no interviews, and hung up.

After cleaning up the breakfast dishes I loaded the kids into the Land Cruiser and drove to the Edgartown police station, which not long before had been the envy of every other town on the island but which now was rivaled by the new Vineyard Haven station. *Sic transit gloria mundi.* I found the Chief in his office.

"Didn't I see you on television the other night?" I asked, while Joshua and Diana wandered around, looking at pictures on the walls and trying out chairs.

"I saw that myself, when I got home. I thought I looked very professional."

"And all you told them was that the cir-

155

cumstances were under investigation. You were very cool."

"Chief Cool, that's me. How's your wife doing?"

"She went to work this morning. How's the investigation going? I know Zee talked with somebody from the D.A.'s office yesterday."

"If I were the D.A., I'd say it was self-defense and drop it, but I'm not the D.A. I'm only a simple small-town cop."

Small-town, yes; simple, no.

"I'm trying to locate a fellow police officer of yours named Graham," I said. "He's working up around Boston. I have a couple of other people looking for him, but I thought maybe you could help, too."

"I work in Edgartown, not Boston. Who's this Graham guy?"

I told him what I'd been told. The Chief listened. When I was through, he said, "Haven't you had enough trouble with Sonny Whelen? My advice to you is to get shuck of this whole business. Where's Rimini right now?"

Technically, I didn't know exactly where he was. Maybe he'd gone for a drive; maybe he was shopping at the A&P. "I don't know," I said.

The Chief studied me, then shook his

head. "You just can't leave things alone, can you?"

"Like I told you, Rimini is married to my ex-wife," I said. "I'm only interested in him because of her. She's a good person and she and their kids don't deserve what's happening to them because of him."

"You're not her husband anymore."

"I know that."

"You've got a family of your own to worry about."

"I know that."

He leaned back in his chair and looked at me. Then he shook his head. "You're a hopeless case, J.W. All right, I'll make a few calls and see if I can track down this Graham guy. But don't get your hopes up that I'll find him." He reached into a drawer of his desk and brought out two lollipops. "Here, kids."

"Thank you," said my well-brought-up children, accepting his offerings.

We got back into the Land Cruiser and went home, where I opened some of the steamer clams Zee had stuck in the fridge, sliced up some onions, and deep-fat-fried an excellent high-calorie lunch for all three of us. Delish! I accompanied mine with two bottles of Sam Adams while the tads drank lemonade.

By the time I'd gotten things cleaned up, I was feeling pretty good, the way you do when your belly's just full enough, but not too full, of tasty food and drink. I put the rest of the clams in the freezer for future reference and, it being a lovely warm day and the tide being right, informed Diana and Joshua that we were going to use the next couple of hours of the afternoon to get ourselves some mussels.

This plan proved popular, so we got into our bathing suits and I loaded buckets and gloves and life jackets for the kids into the old Toyota, and we drove to the landing at Eel Pond, where the mussels thrive.

When Joshua was only a babe, I'd built a floating kid-holder for him out of inner tubes, so he could stay beside me, high and dry, while I went shellfishing. Later, when he was bigger and Diana was just a baby, I'd put her in this same kid-holder and had rigged up a single inner tube that would allow Josh to stand inside it but not fall through. Now both had graduated to regular kids' life jackets, which let them walk on the sand and mud and through the shallow water of the clam-flats, or float over the deep spots.

We walked to the right until we came to the narrows where the little island appears when the tide goes down, and crossed to the far side, me wading, the kids floating and paddling until their feet could reach the mud and sand again.

Eel Pond is full of shellfish: steamers, mussels, quahogs, scallops sometimes, and even some oysters. It has houses on three sides and a beach and an opening to Nantucket Sound on the east. Its entrance is too shallow for any boat with much draft, but small sail- and powerboats are anchored there all summer long, and it's such a popular spot for shellfishing that toward the end of summer the steamers get pretty hard to find. On the other hand, for reasons that elude me but for which I offer thanks to the sea gods, very few people gather mussels from the pond's banks. The result of this policy is that I can get as many as I need anytime I need them, which is very fine since I hold mussels to be the sweetest and tastiest of all the Vineyard's shellfish.

It's easy to get them. All you do is pull them out of the mud beneath the grass that grows on the banks of the pond. They're smaller than most of the mussels you can buy in the A&P, and their shells aren't smooth, but they taste as good as any mussels ever made, and you can get all you want in a half hour.

Unless you have small helpers, in which case it takes longer because you have to keep an eye on them just in case they do any of the possibly dangerous things that you did when you were their age.

Such as wandering around a corner out of sight; or deciding that the far side of the pond, across a couple of hundred yards of over-a-kid's-head water, looks more interesting than the part you're standing on, and is worthy of a visit; or trying to extract a broken beer bottle sticking out of the mud.

These distractions turned a half hour's work into an hour's work, but I didn't really mind because my children's lives interested me, and the slowed-up mussel collecting gave me more time to think about what I was going to do with Tom Rimini's problem. What was increasingly clear to me was that what everyone — Zee, Joe Begay, the Chief, and even Sonny Whelen — had suspected was true: I wouldn't be doing this if it weren't for my feelings about Carla. I didn't know exactly what those feelings added up to, but there was no doubt that they existed and that it was because of them that I wanted to extricate Rimini from the hole he'd dug for himself.

When we finished collecting our mess of mussels, we went for a walk on Little Beach.

All the way down to the lighthouse and back, through June people on towels and under umbrellas, lolling in the summer sun and looking out at the boats leaving and entering the harbor. Diana and Joshua collected some valuable shells that looked to me a lot like many other shells they'd collected in the past, and we all looked for additions to the family beach glass collection, which we kept in jars at home.

Then we went home so I could scrub the mussels clean and put them to soak in salt water overnight, then prepare supper.

When Zee got home, I poured Luksusowa for both of us while she changed into shorts and a tee-shirt, and the two of us went up to the balcony.

The last of the boats were coming in and the cars along the beach were heading home. The warm sun was slanting in from the west onto our backs.

"How are you?" I asked.

"I'll be better tomorrow," she said.

"I'm sorry you aren't today."

"It's okay. Today is just one day too soon, is all."

I must have had question marks all over my face, because she immediately went on.

"When Toni and I talked yesterday, she told me about a custom they have out where

Joe lived in Arizona. She said some of the people out there on the reservation have a tradition of mourning their dead for four days, then getting on with their own lives. This is the fourth day since I shot those men. I think I've been mourning the death of the person I thought I was before that happened. But even though that person is dead, I'm still alive and I've got to get on with it. Today was the last mourning day."

I looked at her, loving her bruised face and her bruised soul and her courage.

"Good," I said, wishing I was as brave.

15

The next morning we woke to the drone of rain on the roof. It was a steady, gray rain, the kind that's great for gardens but not welcomed by tourists who want to spend their Vineyard vacations on the beach.

"Don't go downtown today," said Zee. "It'll be zoo time."

Too true. On rainy days when nobody can go to the beach, the Vineyard's summer people, bound and determined to waste not a moment of their vacation time, all go into the village centers to window-shop and wander around in their raincoats or under umbrellas. The narrow streets of the towns, filled with cars and pedestrians even on sunny summer days, become parking lots when it rains, and natives try their best to stay home until the sun comes out again.

For breakfast, I poured juice for all, milk for the cubs, coffee for the big people, and baked the world's best bran muffins made from the dough we kept ready-mixed in the fridge. I served them with real butter, and I could feel my taste buds jumping up and down with joy.

"Not bad, Pierre," said Zee, wiping her lips. The split one was getting better, I could see, but it was still there, as were the bruises. If there was a hell, I hoped that Pat "The Pilot" Logan was in it. Vindictive me.

"More, Pa?" Diana was a fan of all foods, which made us a lot better off than families with picky eaters.

I gave her another muffin and looked at Zee. "How are you feeling today?"

She smiled. "I may not be quite singin' in the rain, but I'm through wearing black. And now I've got to go to work."

"A working wife is a pearl beyond price."

"And don't you forget it." She grabbed her topsider, kissed us all, and ducked out to her little Jeep.

I watched her disappear up our wet, sandy driveway, and willed her to be past grief as well as past mourning.

"Pa, can I have the last muffin?"

"No, Pa, I want it!"

"No fighting," I said. "You've both had plenty."

"But I'm still hungry."

"Me, too, Pa."

"Me, too," I said. "So we'll split it three ways. Diana gets first choice because she's the littlest, then you get the next choice, Josh, and I go last because the guy who does the dividing always goes last so he'll make an honest cut."

We ate the last muffin and I did the dishes while the rain droned on the roof. I love the sound of rain as long as I don't have to be out in it, and I approve of people who build skylights in their bedrooms just so they can hear the sound of the drops. The roof of our old house was so thin that no skylights were needed. In fact, it was often too thin, as attested to by my routine leak-stopping expeditions over the tar paper shingles.

"Pa, can we go out and play?"

"It's raining, Josh. You'll get wet and cold."

"We'll wear our raincoats and hats, Pa."

I could remember when playing in the rain had been a lot of fun.

"Okay, but come in when you get cold. I don't need any kids with pneumonia."

I got them dressed and out they went. I watched their rain gear turn wet and shiny. They put out their tongues to catch the falling drops and kicked at puddles and ran around in circles. Happiness.

I wasn't running around in circles; I was at a standstill. All I could do for Tom Rimini was try to keep people from knowing where he was until I could get a line on Graham and try to work out some sort of deal with him. Did vice guys give witness protection to small-time gamblers? I didn't know, but I wanted to find out.

I got my first clue about Graham an hour later when the phone rang. It was Quinn, up at his *Globe* desk in Boston.

"I don't know if this guy is the right Graham," he said, "but he's the only Graham anybody seems to know about. This one was a Justice guy, first name Willard, who used to work out of Boston. I don't know what he's doing right now, but a few years back he was with the DEA. Maybe he still is, or maybe he's with some other Justice office or division now. And maybe he's not the same Graham at all."

"I'm looking for a Graham who's interested in gambling, not in drugs."

"They go together sometimes, don't they?"

"Everything goes together sometimes. Ask around some more. See if you can find out what your Mr. Willard Graham is doing these days."

"Unlike you," said Quinn, "I have a job. I can't spend all my time running around chasing ghosts."

"Did I tell you I'm thinking of giving up playing host to bums from Boston who come down here to sponge off me and get me to take them to spots where even they can catch bluefish?"

"They just pretend to come down for the fish. They really come down so your poor wife can have the company of real men for a change. How is your better half, by the way?"

"Better every day."

"Good. Tell her that whenever she comes to her senses and leaves you, I'll be waiting for her up here. She deserves some happiness after all she's been through with you. Meanwhile, I'll poke around Graham's trail a little more, but don't get your hopes up."

He rang off and I called Detective Gordon R. Sullivan, of the Boston PD, and told him what Quinn had told me.

"Well, well," said Sullivan. "Maybe I've been asking the wrong people. I thought Graham was in vice, working on gambling and loan-sharking and like that. I didn't talk with anybody in drug enforcement, but I will. Some of our guys work with the feds, so they might have met him if he's DEA. But if he is, why's he interested in your pal Rimini's gambling problems?"

"You're the detective," I said. "You tell me."

"I'll let you know what I find out. Unless doing that will compromise some operation, in which case you'll get nothing."

"Fair enough. If I hear from you there's no operation; if I don't, there is. Right?"

"More or less."

We hung up and I called Joe Begay. I was having a lucky streak; he was there. I told him what Quinn and Sullivan had told me.

"Willard Graham, eh? I haven't gotten to Willard, yet. I'm working on some other Grahams. Mostly a process of elimination. I need a Graham who's on the job around Boston, and I'm weeding out the ones who don't fit the description. I'll take a shortcut now, and home in on Willard, just in case he's the Graham we're after. I wonder what the DEA finds interesting in a schoolteacher with a gambling habit."

"Me, too."

"I'll call back."

I went out on the porch and watched my now muddy children racing around trying to get as wet as they could. They put their faces up into the rain, they jumped in puddles, they fell down and rolled on the wet grass. The rain fell. They laughed and screamed. Fun!

I went into their rooms and got out dry clothes for them, then poured myself a cup of tea and went back onto the porch. Fun was still happening. Diana got up from the middle of a puddle and came to the bottom of the steps. Her face was white and she was shivering, but she wasn't ready to come in. She and a million other kids were the same way about coming out of the water when their parents can see the goose bumps. So I'm shivering, so I'm freezing, so what?

"Come out, Pa! It's lots of fun!"

"Your teeth are chattering. Time to come in and take a warm shower."

"No!" (Chatter, chatter, shiver, shiver.) "I'm not c-c-cold."

I opened the door. "Come in anyway."

She was shivering too hard to put on her crying face. I put out a hand and helped her up the steps and through the porch door. She was soaked. I undressed her there, dropping her sopping clothing onto the porch floor, then picked her up and looked for her brother. He was on his knees watching the rain hitting the water in the puddle his sister had just vacated. A future aquatic engineer.

I called to him: "I'm giving your sister a warm shower. You're next. Come onto the porch and take off all of your wet things."

"Aw, P-P-P-Pa!"

I carried white and shivering Diana into the bathroom, stood her under a warm shower until her skin had some color and her teeth had stopped chattering, then dried and dressed her and gave her a cup of cocoa, and went out and helped freezing but reluctant Joshua to strip before he slouched into the bathroom and took his own shower.

By the time he had warmed up and gotten dressed, I had all of the wet clothes in the washing machine, had hung the soaked raincoats and hats where they could eventually drip dry, and had emptied the rain boots of their water and stood them upside down to drain.

Being islanders, we naturally had other sets of rain gear, in case we needed them. And as it turned out, we did. Joshua and Diana had just finished second cups of cocoa when Joe Begay called.

"An interesting bit of news," he said. "A guy named Willard Graham used to work for the DEA up around Boston. But a couple of years back he got himself canned, along with some other feds. Some serious questions about missing money. There was a bust and the dealers said they'd had money that Graham and his crew never mentioned in their reports."

"Maybe the dealers were lying to get back at them."

"Could be, but the scuttlebutt is that in the last few years other dealers who got themselves busted by Graham's crew had said the same thing. Nobody could ever prove anything, but Graham's bosses finally decided that two and two didn't equal five. Anyway, the upshot is that Agent Willard Graham is now ex-agent Willard Graham. What do you think of that?"

"Did you get a description of Mr. Graham?"

"I did." He gave it to me. "I can probably get a picture, if you want it."

"I want it."

"I'll have them fax it to you."

"No, you won't. Remember me? The last man in America without a computer or a fax or an answering machine?"

He sighed. "Even us savage redskins have faxes these days. All right, I'll have it sent to me and you can get it here. Come up in a couple of hours."

I went to a window and looked at the rain. Dreary. I wondered why an ex–DEA agent was pretending to be a cop and was hassling Tom Rimini over a gambling problem. One thing was pretty clear: Tom Rimini should be told that Willard Graham was not a cop any longer. I wished I'd gotten a description of Graham from either Tom or Carla, but I hadn't. I went back to the phone and called John Skye's house. No answer. I felt a flicker of worry.

I unlocked the gun cabinet and got out my old .38 S and W police special. I stuck the gun under my belt and pulled my shirt down over it. Then I called Helen Fonseca, Manny's wife, and asked if she'd look after Josh and Diana for a couple of hours.

"Sure, J.W. Bring them right down."

In addition to being Zee's pistol instructor, Manny was the island's premier gunslinger and National Rifle Association member, but he and Helen were both total softies when it came to children, their own or anybody else's.

I collected my offspring, got them and myself into dry rain gear, and trotted us all through the drizzle to the Land Cruiser.

"Where we going, Pa?"

"To Mrs. Fonseca's house. You're going to stay there for a couple of hours while I do some work."

"Why can't we go with you, Pa?"

"Just because. It's big-people work. No kids allowed."

"Can we have ice cream, Pa?"

"Sure. When I pick you up again."

Manny and Helen's house was an old island bungalow. Manny's gun shop was in the basement. Upstairs, the rooms were full of worn, comfortable furniture and good smells. Helen welcomed the kids into her

kitchen and waved me on my way. Good old
Helen.

I got back into the Land Cruiser and
drove to John Skye's house. When I turned
off the asphalt, I studied the driveway.
There were wet tire tracks there that seemed
wider to me than the tracks made by Tom
Rimini's Honda. I unzipped my topsider
and followed the tracks.

Rimini's car was in front of the house
where he'd parked it before. The wider
tracks led down to the doors of the barn.

I looked at the house. Smoke was rising
from the fireplace chimney. I sat in the car
and wondered if I was being overly nervous.
I decided I probably was. I got out and went
up to the door and knocked.

Nothing. I knocked again. I heard a voice
saying something I couldn't understand.
Finally, footsteps came toward the door. I
put my hand under my shirt and stepped to
one side. The door opened and Tom Rimini
stood there, looking flighty, like a deer in
hunting season.

"J.W.! I asked you to call before you came
by." He casually put an arm across the door.

"I did call. Nobody answered."

"Oh." He rubbed his free hand across his
lips. "Oh, yes. I remember hearing the
phone. I was in the john."

I looked over his arm into the house. I saw no one. "I've got some news about Graham," I said. "I think it may interest you."

"Graham? News? What? . . ."

The rain was soaking his shirt. "Let's go inside," I said. "You're getting wet."

He seemed to notice the rain for the first time. "Oh. All right. But just for a minute. I was just going out for some groceries."

Jumpy Tom stepped back into the entryway and I went in after him. I could see a nice fire in the living room fireplace. Very cozy on a drizzly day.

"Now," said Tom, "what's this news about Graham?"

I told him.

"Good Lord," he said. "You mean he's not really a cop? But he had a badge."

"You can buy yourself a badge in Wal-Mart. And when he was a real cop, he wasn't working on gambling and gaming, he was DEA. He was working on narcotics."

"But . . ."

"You're being conned," I said. "I don't know why. Do you?"

He shook his head. "No. I can't imagine. Are you sure about this?"

"I'm going to get a picture of Graham. I'll show it to you. If it's the same guy, we'll at least know that much for sure."

"Yes. Bring it by when you get it. How long will it take you?"

"A couple of hours."

"All right. Come back then. I'll be home from shopping by that time." He stepped toward the door. I glanced at the nice fire, then went out past him. When I was in the Land Cruiser, he waved, then shut the door.

I drove toward the highway until the house was out of sight, then stopped and walked back until I could see it. After a while, Rimini and a woman came out of the house wearing raincoats and walked down to the barn. They opened the big doors and she went inside and backed a newish Ford Explorer out into the yard.

I ran back to the Land Cruiser and drove out to the highway. There was another driveway a hundred yards toward Edgartown. I backed into it and waited. In a few minutes the Explorer came out of John Skye's driveway and turned toward me. When it passed I could see that the woman was alone. I pulled out and followed her.

16

The Explorer went right into Edgartown, the move of a driver who didn't know what village traffic was like during a rainstorm, and immediately was entangled in the snail-paced movement of Main Street traffic. Since I was right behind the Explorer, I got a good look at its license plate.

The Explorer and my rusty Toyota inched down Main with the woman ahead of me looking this way and that way as she realized that she wasn't going to find a parking place anywhere. We loafed along until we got to the four corners, where she took a right on South Water and escaped from the worst of the jam of pedestrians and cars. A couple blocks later, she took another right and eased along Cooke Street before going left on Summer. I stayed about a half a block back and did the same.

I had thought she might be going to a hotel, but as I trailed her along the narrow back streets of the village I decided that she was only getting out of John Skye's house for a while and had hopes of using the time to park and wander around Edgartown just like all the other people under umbrellas. She finally found a spot out beyond the Vineyard Museum and I took a look at her as I drove past. She was an attractive woman in her thirties, and if she had noticed me following her, she gave no indication of it. Her face wore that annoyed expression that people get when it's taken them a long time to do a simple thing like park a car.

If I'd been able to find a parking place of my own, I'd have trailed her on foot in the slight hope of perhaps finding out something useful about her, but I didn't manage that, so I drove to Pease's Point Way and followed it to the police station.

"Didn't I just see you yesterday?" asked the Chief in feigned surprise. "What do you want me to do for you this time?"

"I'm a citizen. I just want you to protect and serve, as usual."

"Emphasis on serve. Well?"

I told him about my discoveries regarding Willard Graham.

"Interesting. If Willard is the right Graham, that changes things. If I don't have to track down Graham anymore, what's your next idea about how I should waste my time?"

"I'd like you to tell me who owns this Ford

Explorer." I gave him the license number.

To my surprise, he didn't even make a wisecrack before he went out of the office, then came back and handed me a piece of paper.

Grace Shepard, aged thirty-five, of Boston's North End, owned the Explorer.

"That help?" asked the Chief.

"Not yet, but it might. Is Grace Shepard on any of your wanted posters?"

"While I was on the wire just now, I checked her out. Nobody wants her for anything. Not even a parking ticket. Are you going to tell me what this is all about?"

"I can't tell you what I don't know."

He shook his head. "You'd worry me if I gave you any thought at all."

"Worry about the traffic downtown, Chief, not about me. Thanks for your help."

I went out, got into the truck, and drove to Aquinnah with the rain slapping against my windshield.

A rainy gray day on the Vineyard has a charm of its own. Once you get out of the village centers there aren't as many people on the roads, the trees and grass are shiny and clean, and the haze makes mysteries of ordinary sights. The world is being born again, washed clean of its sins, given a new start. When the clouds part and float away and the sun rises and burns off the mists, it's again the First Day, and all of us are back in Eden.

Or so it sometimes seems.

Not always, of course.

Joe Begay opened the door before I knocked and I went in. He handed me a photograph. It was of a middle-aged guy with a smile on his face. He looked genial and very ordinary, the sort of man you'd never notice on the street.

"Willard Graham, in person," said Begay. "Here, I got you a couple extra copies, in case you want to spread them around."

"You find any other Grahams in your travels?"

"I found several, but no others that seem to fit the bill. I think this is your guy. Show the picture to your friend Rimini, and then you'll know for sure."

"I will. Did you ever hear of a woman named Grace Shepard?"

"You're full of questions. No, I don't know anybody by that name. Who is she?"

I told him.

"You should be talking with Rimini, not me. You can ask him when you show him this picture."

"I'll do that."

"You want me to ask around, see if anybody knows her?"

"I don't want you to use up all your IOUs. She's from Boston. I'll ask some people up there, first."

"I think Rimini may be trying to pull your strings," said Begay, who, I suspected, had spent a lot of time in shadowlands where many events and people were not as they seemed.

The idea that Rimini was being less than straightforward with me was not a shock. I thanked Joe for his help and drove back down-island.

The rain was getting thinner, but the wind was picking up, making things colder. My heater didn't work very well, but I turned it on anyway. If you use your heater in June, what are you going to do when January gets here? I'd find out in January.

I drove into John Skye's yard. There were no new car tracks leading to the barn. I parked beside Rimini's car. Rimini opened the door of the house and waved me in.

The fire still burned in the fireplace, casting a warm glow out into the living room. I stood before it and pulled a photo of Graham out from under my topsider.

"This the guy?"

Rimini took the photo and gave it a worried look. "Yeah. This is him. Is he the one you told me about? He's really not a cop?"

"No, he isn't. He used to be with the DEA, but they canned him. They couldn't prove it, but they thought he pocketed money he found in drug busts. How did you meet him?"

"He found me. I don't know how. He said he was a cop and he wanted to nail Sonny Whelen. He said that if I didn't help him, he'd take me instead. I was scared, so I did what he said. He'd call me and we'd meet and I'd tell him whatever I'd heard. If he's not a real cop, what's he doing?"

"You tell me."

He rubbed his hands. "I don't know. I can't imagine."

"What did he want to know from you?"

"Oh, what I'd been doing as a bookie. What people had said about payoffs and losses. What I'd heard Sonny say or what other people said about him. That sort of thing. It never made any sense to me. I don't know what he was planning, except that he wanted to get the goods on Sonny. I don't know anything about crime, not really."

He certainly didn't look like he understood crime. He looked like a frightened schoolteacher. It was enough to soften your heart.

"You're pretty good," I said.

"What do you mean?"

"That hand-rubbing routine. That worried expression on your face. You should be onstage."

He stepped away, wide-eyed. "I don't understand you. What are you saying?"

"I mean you're a liar, and a good enough one to have fooled me."

"No."

I held up a hand. "Now your lying is okay with me, but now that I've caught on I don't think I'm going to waste any more time with you. So we'll pack up your gear and put it in your car and you can go sponge off somebody else. If you do as good a job on them as you've done on me, you'll probably be fine."

"I don't know what you mean. I've told you the truth! I've told you everything!"

"You didn't mention Grace Shepard."

He sat down on the couch. "Grace . . . ?" He put a look of confusion on his face and let his voice fade away on a line of question marks.

"You know Grace," I said. "Grace Shepard. She was sitting with you in front of this fire when I came by the first time. Lives in Boston, in the North End. Pretty woman. Thirty-five years old. Drives the Ford Explorer that was parked here in the barn. She's down in Edgartown window-shopping right now. I imagine she'll give you a call later, to see if I'm gone so she can come back. That Grace."

He stared into the fire, then rubbed a hand across his forehead. "I didn't want you to know about her. I didn't want Carla to know. I'm sorry. I was going crazy here. I called her up and asked her to come. She just got here this morning." He looked up at me. "Don't tell Carla. Please."

"What phone did you use when you called her?"

His eyes flicked to the wall phone, but his practiced liar's voice said, "I used the cell phone, just like you said."

I wondered how many women had caught my eye after I had married Zee. A lot. I was married, but I wasn't blind. I remembered the feeling of Carla's body against mine, and the warmth of her kisses.

"Where did you meet her?"

He shrugged. "At a conference. She teaches in town. She and her husband had just broken up. We were both bored out of our minds, so we sneaked off for a drink. You probably wouldn't understand. . . ." His voice was tinged with fatalism.

"When was that?"

"A year or so ago."

A year or so, and Carla knew nothing

about it. Or maybe she did. Maybe that was the reason for the heat of her arms and lips.

"Your private life is your business," I said, "but I can't help you if you keep lying to me. I have to know the truth from you and I won't lie to your wife. You've got to send this woman home. Otherwise, things get too complicated. If you won't do that, you'll have to move out of here and take care of yourself."

His sad face was pleading. "Please. Don't tell Carla. It would make her miserable. It's too late for Grace to leave today, but I'll have her go back tomorrow. And don't make me leave. I'll figure something out in a couple of days, and then I'll be out of your hair. I'm sorry that I held back on you, but I needed Grace and I knew you wouldn't let her stay. Please."

Please. Rimini had used the word more often in a half hour than I do in a week. It is a word a lot of people hide behind, because it gives good shelter.

I looked into the fire, just as my ancestors had no doubt done in their caves. It danced and swirled and hypnotized. There is no greater magic than fire, nothing more eternal.

"Well," I said. "At least I don't have to talk

with Graham about witness immunity for you. I had that in mind."

He tried a joke. "Maybe you can arrange it for him."

I wasn't amused.

17

I picked up the kids and took them home, wishing that the rain would stop. It looked like it might, but not right now. The flowers and veggies and lawn and weeds loved it, but the Jacksons flourished more in sunshine. On the other hand, the dreary day was consistent with my dreary feelings about Tom Rimini.

With a rueful thought about the size of my next telephone bill, I called Quinn. Nobody was at the desk, but an answering machine asked me to leave a message. I left one asking Quinn if he could find out anything about Grace Shepard, then called Detective Gordon R. Sullivan. Gordon was out detecting. Everybody was out but me. I left Gordon the same message I'd left for Quinn. I hung up and thought awhile, then called the offices of the Boston School Committee. After a considerable runaround by various employees of that venerable and highly political institution, I was told that no one by the name of Grace Shepard was teaching in the system.

Hmmmm.

While I waited for somebody to call back,

I made four loaves of white bread, using the recipe from my copy of Betty Crocker's old cookbook, which was held together by duct tape. While it was rising, I made a batch of my spaghetti sauce, of which there is no better, the secret ingredients being a can of cream of mushroom soup and a good shot of Donna Flora's Bean Supreme, which, like onions, improves almost any dish that isn't dessert.

The loaves had just come out of the oven and I had cut three hot thick slices and slathered them with butter for me and the kids, when the phone rang.

Quinn or Sullivan?

Neither. "This is Norman Aylward," said a voice. "I'd like to talk with Mrs. Zeolinda Jackson."

"She's working."

"Brady Coyne asked me to talk with her. I'm a lawyer. I worked with Brady on a few cases before I moved down here."

"I'm J. W. Jackson," I said. "Brady said he was going to put us in touch with an island lawyer."

"That's me. My office is in Vineyard Haven. I think we should all get together as soon as possible so we can get to know one another. Then, if we think we can get along, we can discuss the D.A.'s interest in the incident involving your wife."

"Zee works all day. Are you available in the evening?"

"I can be. Seven o'clock tonight sound okay? I imagine the D.A. is already considering his options."

"Seven it is. Where's your office?"

He told me and we rang off.

It irked me that we even needed a lawyer, but I wasn't surprised. Very odd charges have been brought against people and institutions, and very odd decisions have been made by juries and courts. People who should be in jail aren't and people who shouldn't be are. Our most ancient ancestors, like us, probably noted that even when we think we know what justice is, it eludes us as often as not.

This being the case, lawyers like to remind us that as much as we hate them in the abstract we like to have one on our side when we're headed for court.

I wiped melted butter from my chin and licked my fingers. Yum!

"It's good, Pa," said buttery Diana.

"There's nothing better."

"Yeah, Pa." Joshua nodded.

Such bright children, agreeing with their father without reservation.

"More, Pa?"

"Sure. But we're having spaghetti for supper, so save some room for that."

I cut and slathered another slice for each of us.

Divine! God was probably a baker.

Quinn called just before Zee was scheduled to come home from work.

"I checked our morgue and sure enough I found your girl Grace Shepard. Nothing much, though. Her husband, Ralph, got himself shot to death a while back. They found him sitting in the driver's seat of his own Caddie with a bullet hole above his ear. Shot from the suicide seat, apparently. No perp was ever charged, and the general opinion is that the killing was related, as the kids say."

Related. A street term for "drug-related." I remembered Sullivan mentioning Ralph Shepard.

Quinn went on: "He was a couple of steps up from the street dealers, but nobody seemed to really know for sure. The street wisdom was that he was working for our mutual friend Sonny Whelen, in spite of Sonny's well-known spiel that he has nothing to do with drugs, and that somebody else got rid of Ralph so the somebody could run the drug trade there in JP."

"Jamaica Plain was Ralph's bailiwick?"

"Every town has its share of drugs, including JP."

"Who took over for Shepard?"

"That, I cannot tell you. Maybe the cops know, but I don't. I can tell you for a fact, though, that JP has as good a supplier as ever."

"Do you know anything more about Grace Shepard?"

"The morgue has her as the grieving widow, and that's about it."

"Any children?"

"None mentioned. I didn't cover the story, and the guy who did is working out on the West Coast now. I can try to get in touch with him if you want."

"Any other Shepards around town? Mom or Dad or sibs? Anybody who might know more about what happened?"

"They all expressed shock. Inconceivable that their boy Ralph could be mixed up with drugs. A wonderful man with a lovely wife. Used to be an altar boy. A terrible loss. And like that. You know the story."

Indeed. Every time some slimy character gets himself killed, his family and friends weep and proclaim his sainthood.

I thanked Quinn and told him he could do no more for me at the moment. For this news he thanked me profusely in return on behalf of his bosses who could now hope that he would do some work for them for a change.

I looked at my watch. Time for one more call. I made it to Gordon R. Sullivan. He had just come in. I told him what I'd seen and been told about Grace Shepard.

"Oh, yeah," said Sullivan. "I remember Grace. The weeping widow, though I don't really remember seeing many tears when they planted Ralph. And I don't think she was ever a schoolteacher, either, although maybe she tells people that she is, so she'll have a respectable cover. She wasn't any kind of working wife as far as I know. She and Ralph had a place in the North End, and she's still there. I guess Ralph was well insured or had a nest egg stashed away because Grace hasn't worked since, either."

"You seem to have kept pretty good tabs on her."

"Well, she interests me. One of the rumors, you know, is that Sonny Whelen is sweet on her and that it was one of his boys that knocked off Ralph, so Sonny would have a clear field with Grace."

"Maybe Sonny's paying her rent for her."

"Maybe he is. He can afford it, for sure."

"She must be the forgiving type if she's

hanging around with the guy who knocked off her husband."

"Maybe she's the one who shot Ralph, so she could go with Sonny. It happens in the best families. Actually, rumor has it that Sonny's hotter for her than she is for him. Maybe she likes younger men."

"Quinn told me that Ralph ran drugs for Sonny and that afterward somebody else started running them. Do you know who the somebody is? Do you know if he works for Sonny, too?"

"I don't know who's supplying in JP now, but it isn't Sonny. I hear Sonny would like to get the territory back, but he doesn't confide in me very much, so I'm just guessing."

"Does it strike you that there's a lot of coincidence in these tales I've been collecting? Rimini and his wife live in Jamaica Plain, Sonny Whelen used to run the drug market there until Ralph got himself killed there. Willard Graham puts the strong-arm on Rimini there, Pete McBride follows me there, and Ralph's widow is here now with Rimini, who's hiding out from Sonny, and so forth."

"Maybe Jamaica Plain is the real hub of the universe. Or maybe, like you say, it's all a coincidence."

I tried a Bondism: "Once is coincidence,

twice is happenstance, three times is enemy action."

"You should read a better brand of literature. I admit that it does look like JP is a popular spot with some of the people you've gotten yourself mixed up with. But so what? If not JP, it'd be someplace else. Like the wife's lover said when the husband came home early and found him hiding in the chandelier, 'Everybody's got to be somewhere.' "

"You should get a new joke book. Is Sonny still hot for Grace Shepard?"

"Sonny would tell you that he's a faithful and happily married man with a couple of grandchildren. I have it on pretty good authority, though, that he'd like to be very close to Grace. In fact, if Sonny has a weakness, I'd say it was her."

Ah, the fatal femme. "Does she feel the same way about him?"

I could almost see his shrug. "Who knows? But diamonds are a girl's best friend, as they say. He takes her to fancy places, and somebody's paying for her apartment and that big car of hers."

"Then what's she doing down here with Tom Rimini?"

"The first thing that comes to mind is that Sonny entertains Grace on the side, and

Grace and Rimini entertain each other on the side."

"Dangerous stuff. Sonny isn't a guy you want mad at you."

"He's already pretty mad at Rimini. Probably madder now than before those two thugs got themselves shot up in your front yard. Sonny's lost at least three soldiers in the past couple of years, if you count Ralph, and that can't make him happy."

"Does he get hot or cold when things get tough?"

"Some of each. He didn't get where he is by being stupid, but while he was getting there nobody could tell what he'd do. It was one of the things that made him so scary. You cross him or get in his way and he might wait for months to set you up, or, if it was really personal, he was inclined to run right out and shoot you himself. He's done it both ways, although we can't prove it. Maybe he's psychotic or maybe he's just smart as hell. I don't know."

"He seemed stable enough when I talked to him."

"You weren't a threat. You want some advice?"

"Sure."

"Down your way the state cops handle all homicides. I think you should get in touch with them and tell them what you've told me. What's the name of their head guy on the island?"

"Dom Agganis."

"You talk with Agganis. Whatever's going on is tied to the shootings at your house. Tell him everything and give him my name and number. I'll get in touch with him and with some feds I know up here. Let us handle whatever it is that's happening. You drop out and go back to being a family man."

"Good advice," I said.

"You should take it."

Probably. "I'll talk to Agganis," I said.

I was barely off the phone when Zee came through the door. She looked tired and somber in spite of the split-lipped smile she had put on for her entrance. I told her about the call I'd gotten from Norman Aylward and the appointment I'd made for us to see him.

"So we've finally got a lawyer," she said. "I suppose it had to come sometime. Other people have lawyers, and now we do. All right, I'll go see him."

"I'll go with you."

"No. You stay here with the cubs. This is about me."

I put my hands on her shoulders and looked down into those dark, deep eyes. "If it's about you, it's about me, too."

"Yes," she said, "you're right. It is about both of us. But I'll take care of it."

How many times had I taken it upon myself to attend to some matter affecting us both? More than once, and often without even mentioning it, as though it was my duty as a man, as a husband, and not something I should even consider sharing with my wife. Wives, I suspected, did even more of that in marriages than did their husbands.

"All right," I said. "I'll stay home with the kids."

"You're a good man, Charlie Brown."

Zee was barely out the door on her way to see Aylward when the phone rang. It was Carla.

"I've been so worried," she said. "I can't seem to get in touch with Tom. Oh, I hope nothing's gone wrong. I don't know what the boys and I would do without him!"

I could almost see her tears. "He's safe," I said.

"Please don't let him get hurt. He's like a child sometimes. He does foolish things."

"He thinks he's got some sort of plan that will take a few days to work out. Do you know what it is?"

"No. But please keep him safe. I don't

think I could stand it if anything happened to him. Please, Jeff!"

I felt a great pity for her. Her husband was an unfaithful liar, but she loved him and needed him. I decided I could put my distaste for him aside, at least for another few days.

"All right," I said. "I'll make sure that nothing happens to him." The words tasted sour, but they made her happy.

18

The morning was bright and glittering after the passing of the rain. The new sun beamed down on earth and water. Six days before, Pat "The Pilot" Logan and Howie Trucker had driven into my yard, and my world and Zee's world had changed forever. On the first Sixth Day God had seen everything that he had made, and behold, it was very good. I wondered how he felt about how things were going lately.

The night before, in bed, Zee had told me about her talk with Norman Aylward.

"The first thing you should know is that he wasn't wearing a tie."

"Ah! A good sign."

"The second thing is that he's good-looking and I like him."

"I thought you had eyes only for me."

"You're not too observant, but you're nice. Maybe I should tell you that he had a picture of his wife and three little kids on his desk."

"If I had a desk, I'd have a picture of my wife and two little kids on it."

"We chatted while we checked each other

out and when we both — I, at least — decided we could get along, he told me pretty much what Brady told me over the phone."

"Which was?"

"Don't talk with any reporters and don't talk with any cops or legal types without having him alongside. If anybody has any questions, refer them to him. It sounds like what you read in the newspapers: 'Mr. and Mrs. Jackson referred all questions to her lawyer, Norman Aylward. Mr. Aylward expressed every confidence that the district attorney would find that his client had acted completely within the law, but declined further comment.' "

"Good advice, no doubt. Let's take it."

"He doesn't want us to talk about what happened with anybody else, either, including our friends."

"A little late for that."

"That's what I told him. He said that from now on we should just tell everybody that our lawyer has advised us not to say anything to anybody until after the D.A. decides what he's going to do. I told him about the assistant D.A. snake I talked with. He said he didn't know him, but that it was the snakes who are responsible for all those lawyer jokes. I think you'll like him."

I actually did like at least one lawyer:

Brady Coyne. Was it possible for one person to like two lawyers in only one lifetime? What's the difference between a lawyer and a rattlesnake? The snake warns you. Page 1000, volume fifty, of the *Lawyer Joke Book*.

"Do you feel better, having talked with him?"

"Yes. When you think you might be in trouble, even though you don't think you deserve to be, it's nice to know that somebody is on your side."

True.

"Enough of lawyers," she said. "You're the somebody on my side that I'm interested in right now." She rolled toward me and ran her hand down over my belly.

I tried to avoid the scar on her side, but I made good contact with the rest of her and she with me. As I've often said, bachelors are a sad lot.

In the morning, after Zee, looking healthier, drove to work, I packed up Josh and Diana, and followed her to Oak Bluffs. But instead of going to the hospital, I went to the State Police offices on Temahigan Avenue. In past years the building had been painted a dubious shade of blue, but now it was shingled with cedar and looked more Vineyardish.

I parked, and the kids and I went inside

where I was pleased to actually find Corporal Dominic Agganis and not his testy fellow officer Olive Otero. Not that Dom Agganis and I were bosom buddies, but at least we'd gone fishing together and had occasionally shared a beer.

"Well, well," said Agganis, "what brings you to these hallowed halls?"

"Talk."

He opened a drawer of his desk. "You kids want some candy? I've got some lemon drops in here." He brought them out.

"Thank you," said my polite children, holding out their hands.

Agganis took a good look at the Band-Aid on Diana's throat. "What sort of talk? How's your wife, by the way?"

"Better."

"Good. You want your kids to hear this conversation you have in mind?"

I found a chair. "It may bore kids to hear grown-ups talk, but I don't think it hurts them."

He leaned back in his chair. He was a tall, thick-bodied man who usually wore an air of polite skepticism about the world in general. He was very smart and tough. "Well, then."

I told him almost everything I had seen and heard since I'd come home from clamming the morning Logan and Trucker had been shot. I didn't mention the pencil I'd shoved up Trucker's nose or the place where Rimini was staying, but gave him the rest of it, including Gordon R. Sullivan's telephone number. It took a bit of time, but Agganis never interrupted. When I was done, I gave him a copy of the picture of Graham and waited.

"Pa, can we look around?"

"It's not my house, Joshua."

"Sure you can," said Agganis. "Look anywhere you want. Here." More lemon drops exchanged hands and more thank-yous were uttered.

"Stay together," I said, "and don't touch anything."

"Yes, Pa."

Agganis watched them ease into a hallway. "How's the little girl?" he asked, touching his throat with a thick finger.

"She only got a small cut. I don't think she gives it a thought. Kids may be little, but they're tougher than you'd think."

"Where's Rimini hiding out?"

I'd been sure he'd ask. "Do you have to know?"

"He's in the middle of something that's already got one man killed and another all shot up. He's got Sonny Whelen looking for

202

him already, he's got this Graham character pulling his strings, and now he's got the woman who may be Sonny's girlfriend down here with him. Because of him, your wife had to kill a man and your daughter damned near got her throat cut. I'd say there's plenty of reason for me to know."

"The more mouths, the fewer secrets."

"Don't irk me, J.W."

"He's at John Skye's farm. You know where that is?"

"Yeah. Up off the Edgartown–West Tisbury Road."

"John and Mattie and the twins are out West for a month. I look after the place, so I stuck him there until I could figure out what else to do with him."

He nodded. "It's a good spot to hide somebody, but I get the impression that Rimini's not as keen on being hid as you are on hiding him. He's already brought in this bird from Boston. Who else knows where he is?" He tapped his fingers on his desk. "I think this Sullivan guy up in Boston is right. I think you'd better step out of this dance and let the authorities handle things from now on."

"I have some interests the authorities don't have."

"Yeah. Rimini's wife."

He could be snide when it pleased him. So could I. "I don't want her to get hurt, but I don't think the authorities you mention give a damn about her one way or another."

"You interfere with an investigation, you'll end up in court." He waved his trigger finger at me.

I waved mine back. "Yeah, but there isn't any investigation to interfere with. None of those authorities you talk about are investigating Rimini."

He had a little smile that consisted of one corner of his mouth lifting in what also looked like a sneer. "Don't bet your life savings on that, not that you have any life savings. I'm still investigating the shooting at your place, and Rimini is in the middle of it."

"Let's have some tit for tat," I said. "I've told you what I know, now you tell me what you know."

The smile became bigger. "You jest."

I didn't have any smile at all. "No. My wife and daughter almost got killed. Trucker told me it happened because Whelen sent them to get Rimini, and Logan let his testosterone get the best of him. Whelen sort of halfway told me that sending Trucker and Logan after Rimini was a mistake, but he never actually said that he sent them. He told me that Trucker and Logan were already on the island, vacationing with their wives, when they got the job. Did you talk with the wives? Are they still here? Where? Can you make Whelen as the mastermind?"

"You're full of questions, aren't you? Well, I'll tell you this much: Logan's widow and Trucker's wife and all of their kids who were here on vacation are off the island now and back home in America. The women claim they don't know a thing about their hubbies' work, and that may be true, since a lot of hoods keep their professional lives and their family lives separate, and a lot of hoods' wives go out of their way not to know anything and to keep their kids from knowing anything about their men's business. As far as I know, the same goes for Sonny Whelen's family. They may know his reputation from what they read in the papers and hear on the news, but then again maybe they don't read, or watch TV."

"Where were Logan and Trucker staying?"

"Why? You want to go search the places for clues? Save your energy. Trucker owned a house up in Chilmark. We got a warrant to search the place, but we didn't find a thing and the wives didn't leave anything of theirs behind. No confessions, no incriminating letters from Sonny Whelen, no nothing. Forget it."

"Can you tie this to Sonny any tighter than I have?"

"Not yet, but when you get yourself out of the picture there'll be one less person blocking the view."

"Dom, if it wasn't for me coming here today, you wouldn't have any idea that this whole thing wasn't just Sonny Whelen muscling Rimini over a gambling debt."

"And you think it's more than that?"

"Yes."

"Okay, smart guy, tell me. You tell me what's going on and then we'll both know."

"I don't know."

"I didn't think so."

"Pa, there's goldfish. Come and see. Come and see, Pa." Diana waved an arm, beckoning.

I got up, looking at Agganis. "You have goldfish? I didn't know authorities kept goldfish."

"Yes, we have goldfish. There's a lot you don't know about authorities."

He got up and went down the hall with Diana and me. In the next room was a small aquarium containing several varieties of fish, most of them goldfish. We all stood and admired them.

"Can we have some goldfish, Pa? Look at that one. She's my favorite."

"Maybe we can have some little fish," I said. "I'll think about it."

"Sure you can have some," said Agganis. "Your dad knows how much you want some, so he'll get them for you. Isn't that right, J.W.?"

I gave him a sour look.

"Can we, Pa? Can we?"

"We'll see."

"You can buy them right here in town at the tackle shop," said Agganis.

"Come on, kids, it's time to go. See you later, Dom."

"Come back anytime, kids. You, too, J.W."

We went out to the truck.

"Can we have a dog, too, Pa?"

"No. No dogs."

"Can I have my very own goldfish?"

"Me, too, Pa? I want my own goldfish, too."

"We'll see."

I took Barnes Road to the Vineyard's only blinker, crossed the highway and took Airport Road to the end, then took a left toward Edgartown. When I got to John Skye's driveway, I pulled off the road.

"Stay here. Don't get out of the truck. I'll be right back."

"Okay, Pa."

I walked down the driveway until I could see the buildings through the trees, and found myself a shady nook behind a scrub oak. Rimini's car and Grace Shepard's big Explorer were parked side by side.

Grace clearly hadn't taken an early boat back to America. While I was watching, she and Rimini came from the house and went to the Explorer. They looked around in that way people have when they don't want to be seen, then took some gear from the Explorer's rear compartment and carried it back to the house. Two of the items looked like cases for rifles or shotguns. After a while they came out again. Rimini walked down to the barn and opened the double doors. Grace Shepard drove the Explorer into the barn, then came out. She helped Rimini shut the doors and they both walked back to the house.

I didn't think I was going to see much else, so I went back to the Land Cruiser.

"Pa."

"What?"

"Can we have some other kinds of fish, too? Like we saw today?"

"We'll see."

I drove us home and fixed us some lunch. While I did, I thought of the renewed promise I'd given to Carla to take care of her errant husband. A promise made is a promise kept, but Rimini was making this one hard. I felt tightened muscles in my jaw.

19

John Skye was an occasional shooter of ducks and geese. Sometimes he'd come down during bird season and spend some hours in a blind out on the Edgartown Great Pond. For several years I went with him, and we had gotten our share of game; but then our passion for shooting seemed to wane at about the same rate, and our last hunts had consisted mostly of sitting, freezing, in our blind, drinking coffee laced with brandy, munching sandwiches, gossiping, and watching ducks sail over us and our unfired guns.

I had no moral objection to hunting, holding as I did to the proposition that if you ate it you could shoot it, whether in season or out. If a man with a hungry family jacked a deer or potted himself an out-of-season duck or two, he wouldn't get reported by me. On the other hand, I, like John, rarely enjoyed even a good killing shot, so had pretty much given up hunting altogether.

But I still had my father's deer rifle and shotguns locked in our gun cabinet, and in the wintertime I kept John's long guns there as well, just in case some local thief broke into his house when I wasn't around.

Now, drinking Sam Adams beer, and sharing ham-and-cheese sandwiches made from yesterday's fresh-made bread, I watched my children eat and considered the sight I'd just seen in John Skye's yard.

One reading of it was that from the beginning Tom Rimini had been far more frightened than I'd thought. Not content to simply hide out until some resolution of his dilemma could be determined, he felt the need of weapons to protect himself. If that was the case, he must have been a lot more interested in John's gun cabinet than in the fine library I'd imagined he'd value when I first took him out to the farm. He must have perked right up when he'd first seen the cabinet, but been sorely let down when he found it to be unlocked and empty.

That might explain a desperate call to Grace Shepard. Her husband, having been in the dangerous business of supplying drugs, no doubt had weapons, and she, now Rimini's mistress, apparently had been willing to bring some of them down to her lover.

In this scenario, he'd called her because he wanted her with him and he wanted weapons, but he hadn't wanted me to know about any of that because he was still dependent on me to keep him safe and he knew I'd be angry with him if I discovered his betrayal of our agreement, to say nothing of his betrayal of his wife.

And he'd been right. I had been angry, but I'd been mollified by his promise to send Grace back home, and by my own disquieting realization that even after years of separation, and in spite of my marriage to Zee, I still found Carla attractive and still cared about what happened to her.

But he hadn't mentioned the guns, and he hadn't sent Grace back. He'd lied.

Why?

Because he loved Grace Shepard more than he loved Carla, and was more afraid of Sonny Whelen than he was of me?

Maybe.

What would I have done if I were in his predicament, feeling the way he did? Maybe the same thing.

But I wasn't him and never would have been.

"More, Pa?"

Diana the Huntress, licking her fingers, always after food.

I made another sandwich, cut it in two, and gave half to her and half to Joshua.

"Thank you, Pa."

"You're welcome."

Why had Grace brought long guns to Rimini instead of pistols? Because Rimini, like most men, wasn't a short-range shootist and didn't know much about handguns? Even cops, who carry side arms and are trained to shoot, and whose jobs bring them up against society's most violent people, don't know a lot about handguns, are notorious for being bad shots when shoot they must, and usually retire without ever having fired their pistols anywhere except on a range. Most Americans don't shoot at all, and if they do it's because they're hunters, like John Skye, who shoot rifles and shotguns. If they have any training whatsoever, it's usually the rifle practice they got in the armed services. So, if Rimini was a normal guy who suddenly thought he needed a weapon, he'd go for a long gun, if he went for any gun at all.

But unless my eyes had deceived me, he and Grace had carried at least two gun cases into the house. Why the need for more than one weapon? Was Grace the loyal gun moll? Was she going to stand shoulder to shoulder with her man and blow the bad guys away as they came through the windows? And even if that was the plan, did they really expect Sonny Whelen to come busting in, guns blazing? Or Sonny's men, if not Sonny himself?

Or did Rimini fear someone else? Graham, maybe? Was Graham after his scalp for some reason? If so, why?

Or was it somebody else entirely? Pete McBride and his muscle, Bruno, maybe.

But if Pete McBride was after Sonny Whelen's throne, why would Pete come gunning for Tom Rimini, who was at best a very small cog in a very big machine?

I emptied my beer bottle.

The thing was that none of those guys were supposed to know where Rimini was hiding out. They knew that he was on the Vineyard somewhere, but even the Vineyard, small as it looks on maps, consists of something like 130 square miles of land, most of it still pretty undeveloped; finding Rimini would be like finding the proverbial needle.

Unless Rimini, frightened and alone, had somehow revealed his location.

I wouldn't put it past him to have done exactly that. He'd definitely called Grace, and maybe Grace really liked Sonny's attentions more than Rimini's. Maybe she'd tipped Sonny off, then come down to sucker Rimini into thinking she was on his side. She'd have brought the guns he'd asked for, but maybe that was just to get him feeling good, so she could liquor him asleep, and then open the door to Sonny's men.

Or maybe he planned to shoot me.

There was a thought. Maybe I was the weak link as far as he was concerned. If he got rid of me, nobody would know where he'd gone. Nobody, that is, but Zee and the kids. And, of course, Dom Agganis; but Rimini didn't know about Agganis, so as far as he was concerned, only the Jacksons could lead Sonny to John Skye's farm. I tried but failed to see Tom Rimini as a mass murderer. I also tried and failed to see myself as always being right about people. I had been fooled before and would no doubt be fooled again.

Whatever Rimini was up to, I didn't like those long guns, and I didn't like his lies. I called Helen Fonseca and asked if she could take the kids for an hour in exchange for some bluefish pâté. She said she'd take them for nothing, but would never say no to bluefish pâté since Manny was a hunter but not much of a fisherman.

I took the kids and the pâté to Manny's house, told Helen that I was forever in her debt, and drove to the police station. The Chief wasn't in; he was downtown directing traffic. Since it was a lovely, sunny day, Edgartown was only half as mobbed as it had been during the rain and I managed to find a parking place on Summer Street. The Chief was standing in front of the Bickerton and Ripley Bookstore, watching a summer cop try to keep traffic flowing and pedestrians from being run over. No easy task, but the girl was not doing too badly, all in all.

"Nobody's been killed since I got here," said the Chief. "I'm a good teacher."

"Some were born to lead," I said.

"I know you want something. What is it?"

"I need to confess my sins, and since I don't go to church I decided to come to you as the closest thing to a priest, or a father figure, at least."

"I don't think we have time to discuss all of your transgressions, so let's just talk about one or two of the worst of them."

I told him about my talk with Agganis and what I'd seen since at John Skye's place.

"Rimini lied to me about Grace Shepard, and he never told me about those long guns. Maybe he lied about other stuff, too. I thought I knew what was going on, but now I'm not so sure."

"This isn't the first time you've thought wrong."

"Mea culpa, mea culpa. The thing is, so far the only crime Rimini's admitted committing has been taking bets in Boston. He hasn't broken any laws on Martha's Vine-yard unless he isn't licensed to have those guns."

"Maybe he lied to you about his gambling problems, just like he lied about this Shepard woman and the guns."

I nodded. "Yeah, but why would he do that? He was running from Sonny Whelen for some reason, and Sonny was mad enough to send those goons to my house looking for him."

"Too bad Sonny didn't take that job him-self. Zee could have plugged the head of the mob instead of just a couple of soldiers."

"Tsk, tsk, Chief. That's a very unlawmanlike sentiment."

"I have a lot of unlawmanlike sentiments, several of them having to do with you. I'll check and see if Rimini has a firearms' permit. If he doesn't, I suppose I can go up there and arrest him for illegal possession, but if he does, I don't think there's anything I can do about him, except let him know that the local law has its eye on him. If he has something illegal in mind, that may keep him from doing it."

"Blessed are the peacekeepers."

"I don't know how many people have advised you to step out of this affair and leave it to the pros, but you can add me to the list."

"I think you're either number three or number four," I said.

"You're going to accept our counsel, of course."

"I probably should," I said, and crossed the street barely fast enough to avoid being run over by a car driven by a lady who was admiring something in a store window. The summer cop blew her whistle just in time to stop the car from hitting her. The driver looked embarrassed when the cop stared at her through the windshield then waved her on down Main. The Chief, watching all this, didn't change expression. Another triumph for law and order.

I found a phone and called John Skye's house. After three rings, Rimini picked up the receiver.

"Yes?"

I told him I was coming out.

"When?"

"In about two minutes."

"Oh. Oh, all right."

I hung up, found my truck, and drove to the farm. It took a lot longer than two minutes, but I hoped my lie would keep Grace Shepard from trying to drive away before I got there.

It did.

Rimini opened the door of the house when I drove into the yard, and stepped out onto the front porch. No rifles or shotguns were in sight. Neither was Grace Shepard, but a moment later she moved into view behind Rimini.

Rimini looked nervous, but Grace looked cool.

"I know what you're thinking," said Rimini as I got to them. "I can explain."

"You're Grace," I said to the woman.

"Yes." She put out her hand and smiled. "You're Mr. Jackson. How do you do?"

She wore Bermuda shorts, sandals, and a blouse that complemented her hair and complexion. Summer wear for Martha's Vineyard. She had a good figure and her face was smooth and well-featured. Her blue eyes were keen and, at that moment, inquisitive. It wasn't hard to imagine why more than one man had found her attractive. She was the kind of woman who could have a man anytime she wanted, and probably any man she wanted.

"I heard that you were going to be back on the mainland by now," I said.

"You were misinformed, I'm afraid. You aren't going to make an issue of it, are you?" She smiled a smile that could change a lot of minds.

"I'm not," I said, "but Sonny Whelen might, if he finds out."

20

"What do you mean?" asked Rimini in a startled voice. His eyes flicked to the woman's face and then back to mine. "Do you know something? How . . . ?"

"Take it easy, dear," said the woman, putting a hand on his arm. "Don't jump to conclusions. I'm sure Mr. Jackson will explain what he means." The blue eyes looked up into mine. "You will, won't you? I'm afraid that Tom's a little on edge these days. You can understand why a remark like yours could disturb him."

"It's pretty simple," I said. "Tom, here, isn't the only guy who has eyes for you. Sonny Whelen does, too. In fact, I'm told you're a weakness of his. He's already after Tom and if he finds out you're down here with him, he'll have two reasons for being mad. He might even be mad enough to come down here himself, since they say he likes to handle personal matters personally."

"But who would tell him, Mr. Jackson? Not you, surely. Not after the efforts you've made on Tom's behalf? And if not you, then who?" She now had both hands on Rimini's arm, and was holding him close to her, as if to protect him from the evils of the world.

"No, I wouldn't tell him," I said, trying and failing to see past those sharp blue eyes into her mind, "but I know a couple of people who might: Tom's wife, for one. They put the fear of God into her before, and they might do it again."

"But she doesn't know where he is."

"Don't count on it. Tom, here, told you, didn't he? How many other people has he told?" I looked at him. "He has a hard time keeping things to himself."

"I didn't tell anyone but Grace!" cried Rimini. "She's the only one!"

"You wouldn't hold back on me, would you, Tom?"

"No! I'm telling you the truth."

"All of it?"

"Yes."

"How about you, Mrs. Shepard? Are you telling me all of the truth, too?"

She smiled. "No woman ever tells any man all of the truth, Mr. Jackson."

I liked her brass, and saw still more clearly how she could be a magnet for men. "That's not the kind of truth I'm talking about, Mrs. Shepard."

"What kind are you talking about, Mr. Jackson?"

I looked from one to the other. "We can start with the guns. Neither one of you has mentioned them."

Rimini paled, and something in his eyes became feral, but the woman only shrugged.

"They belonged to my husband. Tom is pretty nervous, so I brought them down when I came. Maybe he didn't mention them because he didn't think they were important. You might think of them as props, psychological props."

"If you want protection, you should call the cops."

Rimini started rubbing his hands. "No. No police. I may have something worked out. I just have to think about it some more. Grace is right. She brought the guns because I've been frightened. Why, we don't even know how to shoot. I haven't touched a weapon since I got out of basic training. It's just that . . ." He let his voice trail away, then shook his head. "I don't think you can understand. You've never been afraid. You've never had killers after you."

I had bullet and shrapnel scars that said he was wrong, but saw no point in mentioning them since he was totally caught up in his own situation.

"What's this plan you're working on?"

He shook his head. "It's too soon to talk

about it, but in a couple of days I'll know. I'll tell you when I've got it figured out. I need to stay here until I do. Is that all right? I want Grace to stay, too. I need her."

He was a fairly pitiful sight, with those nervous hands and wild eyes. He seemed to be one of those men who needed a woman who was stronger than he was, and Grace struck me as fitting that bill. I had little feeling for Rimini, but I felt sorry for Carla and their sons. Rimini was a poor figure of a husband and father.

Grace Shepard stepped forward. "If we can just be alone for two or three days, I'm sure we can resolve Tom's problem. Tom and I have to talk things out without anyone else being around. You've been wonderful to Tom, and I know that you've got a major interest in what happens to him, but if you can just leave us alone here for two or three days, I promise you that we'll get everything worked out and get out of your life."

Her blue eyes were wide and full of arcane intelligence. She put one hand on my arm. "Please. Just two or three days. We need that much time for Tom to calm down and for the two of us to talk. Then we'll be gone."

"Show me the guns."

"Certainly." She led me into the library. There, on a reading table surrounded by shelves filled with thousands of John Skye's books, were two gun cases. I opened them and found a 30.06 Winchester and a Remington 12-gauge pump gun. Two common weapons.

"Your husband was a hunter, Mrs. Shepard?"

She nodded. "He used to go to Maine with friends. I'm afraid I don't know much about guns." She pointed to a satchel. "I brought bullets, too, but I'm not sure they're the right ones. They were in the closet where Ralph kept the guns."

I opened the satchel. The ammunition was for these weapons. There was also a box of 9-mm ammunition for a pistol that wasn't there. Ralph apparently hadn't had a chance to use his nine when he'd been shot.

"Where's the pistol that goes with this?" I asked.

The woman shook her head. "I don't know. I didn't know Ralph had a pistol."

I zipped the gun cases. "I advise you just to leave these weapons alone. Pretend you don't even have them. If, for some reason, you think you're in danger, call the police."

She glanced back toward Rimini, who was standing in the adjoining room, and lowered her voice. "I will. Tom doesn't want the police involved because of his own gambling, but I'll call them if we need protection. I'd rather have Tom alive and in jail than dead. I won't take any chances."

"Good. I'll be back in a couple of days. Good luck with the master plan." I could hear the sarcasm in my voice.

Her smile was not free of mockery. "Thanks. And thanks for being understanding. Tom is a wonderful man, but his nerves have gotten bad; still, with your help I think we'll be fine."

Maybe Tom and Grace would be fine, but I doubted if Carla's situation was going to improve.

When I passed Rimini on my way out, all I managed to say to him was, "Call your wife every day. She's foolish enough to love you."

I got into the truck, drove to town and picked up the kids, and went home. I was irritated and uneasy, but my discontent was not made glorious by any sun, for there was only darkness where my thoughts and feelings dwelled.

If I were a Zen master, I could accept all things, but I am not, and am therefore distressed when some bell rings wrong in my psyche, when my sense is that things are out of joint. And there was something going on with Rimini that illed my ease. The lies and deceptions were part of it, but both my twentieth-century cynicism and my work as a cop had conditioned me, like Sam Spade, to expect people to lie under pressure. I did it myself, after all, from time to time, and Rimini was being pressed hard, so I wasn't shocked. But I was very uneasy.

I went out to the flower beds and popped dead heads and weeded. Overhead the innocent sun shone bright in a clear blue sky. All around me Nature continued her timeless cycle of life and death, ignoring human notions of right and wrong. The great circle rolled and universes disappeared and were created. Neither Rimini nor I would be noted for our coming or our passing. Part of me knew that my worries were absurd, that everything was perfect, that only my human pettiness denied me that realization; but I was stuck with that pettiness and could not set it aside.

A monk went into the wilderness and swore he would not return to the temple until he achieved enlightenment. Years later, having finally seen the white light, he returned. On the way, he met a novice.

"Do you know me?" asked the monk.

"Oh yes," said the novice, "You're the monk who knows everything." And he walked on by.

The phone rang.

"I'll get it, Pa." Joshua galloped into the house.

"I want to get it next time," said an aggrieved Diana, her mouth sagging.

"No sniveling," I said. "Joshua gets it this time; you get it the next time."

"I got it for Ma when those bad men were dead."

"I know. It's just that there are two kids here and only one phone, so you have to take turns. Next time it's your turn."

Joshua came out with the phone in his hand. "It's Quinn."

I took the receiver.

"It's migration time," said Quinn. "I don't know if it has anything to do with you, but Sonny Whelen and some of his minions have dropped out of sight."

"Who?"

"Sonny himself, for one. And Sean. And Todd. Remember him, sitting there with Sonny? I don't think he liked you very much."

"I remember."

"And Pete McBride and his pal Bruno. I think you met them, too."

"Sounds like good news for the Boston PD. Everybody's leaving town. Maybe they've all decided to retire to Florida."

"Sure."

"Where did they go?"

"I don't know, and neither do my contacts in the law enforcement business."

"When did it happen?"

"I just found out about it this afternoon. As far as I know, they were all in town yesterday. People are running around like chickens with their heads cut off. It's not a good feeling when your prime criminal element just disappears."

"Another one of those Mafia conventions like I used to read about? A summit meeting in the Catskills?"

"Could be. I don't know and neither does anybody else. But since you and your friend Rimini have been in Sonny's face lately, I thought you might be interested."

I was interested, all right.

"Do you think they're coming here?"

"Your guess is as good as mine, pal."

"Thanks, Quinn."

I rang off and called Boston's Finest, Gordon Sullivan. He was out. I left a message to call me as soon as he got in. If the Whelen gang had dropped out of sight, I wanted to know if they were headed for the Vineyard.

Then I got out my old .38, checked it, loaded it, and shoved it under my belt.

21

When Zee got home, I waited until she'd changed and played with the kids and the two of us were on the balcony with cocktails. There, I told her everything I'd seen and heard that day.

"Time for you to get untangled from all of this," said Zee. "I don't like the way it smells."

"Neither do I. What does your nose tell you?"

She touched her healing lip with her fingers. "You're dealing with liars, deceivers, and professional criminals. Everybody has a gun. One man is dead already and that was just the start of it all."

"It started before that."

"I meant for us. It started for us then. I'm glad you told the cops about Tom Rimini. They're the ones who should take charge of him, not you."

"I'm not in charge of him, I'm just trying to help him."

"Why? So he can go back home and keep cheating on his wife while he caters to his gambling habit?"

Touché.

"Maybe if we can get him free from Sonny Whelen, he can get into a program. Gamblers Anonymous, or whatever they call that outfit."

"Do they have a Mistress Anonymous he can join? Something for people who can't stay away from other women?" Her voice was sharp.

"They probably do," I said, "but I'm not his social worker, I'm just trying to help him out."

"Because of Carla!"

"I'd like to think I'd help out anybody in a similar jam. I don't want to be somebody who just stands by and watches somebody else get killed."

"Do you love her?"

"I love you."

"But do you still love her, too?"

I'd thought enough about that question, but I still couldn't answer it the way I wanted to. "I have feelings for her. I care about what happens to her. I don't love her like I did when we were married, but she and I shared too much for me to abandon her now."

She stared out over Sengekontacket Pond, but I wasn't sure she was seeing the departing beach people or the boats heading in for the night. Finally, she nodded a small nod. "Yes. That's you, all right. You don't abandon people. I'm sorry. It's just that I don't like this mess we're in, and I don't want it to get worse."

I found her nondrinking hand and gave it a squeeze. "If there's any trouble, I'll try to stay out of it."

"That pistol in your belt says differently."

"Well, you know what Manny Fonseca says . . ."

In ironic unison we recited the gun toters' maxim: "It's better to have one and not need it than to need it and not have it."

"The terrible thing about that," said Zee, "is that it's true. Did I tell you that I gave a blood sample to the D.A. today?"

I felt my muscles tighten. "Was Norm Aylward there?"

"Yes."

I relaxed a bit. "Why do they need a sample of your blood?"

"Because there was a lot of blood around here last week, and they want to know whose was whose. I need to have you tell me something."

"What?"

"Do you really still love me?"

I was surprised. "Let me count the ways."

"No, Jeff, I'm serious. Do you?"

"Of course." I studied her. "You never have to ask."

She shook her head. "I have to because I'm different now. I'm not the person I was a week ago. I don't feel the same. I don't know how anybody can love me, now that I've killed a man."

Such guilt irked me. "I killed a woman and you love me."

"I know, but . . ."

"You'll get past it. Remember, your four days of mourning are over and your life goes on."

"I'm not a Navajo. It's taking me longer."

"Everyone knows you're no killer, and everyone who loved you before loves you still. Look down there." I pointed to Joshua and Diana, who were playing with Oliver Underfoot and Velcro. "You know the kids love you just the same. So do I. So do your friends."

She looked at her children. "Yes." Then she sat back and said, "I think I'm going to give up shooting. It was just a game before, but now it seems like practice for homicide."

"Fine. Manny Fonseca is going to be sad, because you were his best pupil, but he'll understand."

"What a drudge I am," she said. "Full of gloom." She donned a smile and showed it to me. "No more of that."

I wished that I could just accept the smile and play along with it, but I couldn't.

"I'm worried about the Whelen crew disappearing like they have," I said. "I don't know where they went, but one of the possibilities is that they're coming here. It could be that Sonny's got a line on where Tom Rimini is, in which case Tom is in trouble. Or it could be that Sonny's changed his mind about you and me and has decided to stop the laughs about what happened to Logan and Trucker. I think it might be a good idea if you and the kids went up to Aquinnah for the next couple of days."

The smile went away faster than it had come. "Fat chance of that! This is our house, and I won't have anybody running us out of it!"

Tyger! Tyger! burning bright . . .

"It might be safer," I said.

"This is our house! I won't change our life because of some Boston thugs!" She saw something in my face and put both hands on her cheeks. "Oh, my! What am I saying?"

"You're saying that He who made the lamb made thee. . . . And you're right. You're the gentlest person I know, but when there's a threat to your family, you turn into a lioness." I felt my head tip to one side as I looked at the fire deep in her bottomless eyes. "Some people call it maternal instinct, but you had it in you before we had children, so I call it love."

She shook her head. "Is that what it is?"

"Would you die for me?"

"Of course. What a question!"

"And I for you. Would you die for the kids?"

"Yes, of course."

"And so would I. The other side of that coin is fighting for them, if you have to. You did that a week ago and you're willing to do it again. Accept that. I have. If people will leave us alone, they have nothing to fear from us. If they try to hurt us, they put themselves in harm's way. We're together on this."

"Yes. What a world we live in."

What a world, indeed. It was magnificent and grand and beautiful and totally without mercy or meaning.

"So, we'll stay put," I said.

"Yes, but this place is a terrible fort, you know."

When had she studied defensive architecture? "You're right; it's a house, not a castle, but it's not the worst fortress in the world, either. I can't imagine any big-city thugs finding their way here through the trees, so there's only the driveway to bring them in.

Logan and Trucker got here because you never expected an attack. If you plan for one, you've got the edge. You can split, because you know the lay of the land, or you can waylay them on their way in. The defense always has the edge, at least in the beginning."

"I know the first thing we should do: we should call the Chief and have one of his guys stand out there at the head of the driveway!"

"A good thought, but a very expensive one. It costs a lot of money to hire a cop, and we can't afford it."

"We can't not afford it if Sonny Whelen is coming!"

"But we don't know that he is. In fact, if I was to bet on it, I'd say he wasn't. He as much as admitted he'd made a mistake sending Logan here, and he can't like the bad press and the jokes that came out of it. I don't think he wants anything more to do with you or me."

"Are you sure?"

I've been sure about a lot of things that turned out differently from how I expected.

"I'm fairly sure," I said, "but I'll talk with the Chief and Dom Agganis and tell them what Quinn's told me. I think the Chief will be willing to keep an eye on us for the next couple of days, at least."

"Until Tom Rimini and that woman have gone."

"Yes."

"I wish they were already gone."

"Me, too."

Below, on the lawn, the children, green and golden in the heydays of their lives, played with the cats, rubbing their bellies and petting them. Eden, before the fall.

"I'll talk with the Chief right now," I said, finishing my drink.

Downstairs, I called his office. He'd gone home. I called his home and got his wife, who handed him the phone.

"What?"

I told him what Quinn had told me and of my worries.

"You're right to be worried," he said. "You get yourself into these situations and you never learn."

"You really should have been a priest. You love to preach."

"We get paid the really big bucks to protect and serve. I'll call Dom Agganis and see if he knows what's going on. Probably he doesn't because probably Sonny and his gang have all gone up to New Hampshire or Maine or someplace where Sonny doesn't have to read any more stories about how your wife wiped out two of Boston's baddest. How did your pal Quinn learn about this disappearing act, anyhow?"

"He has police sources, he says. You can ask him yourself, if you want to."

"Sure. And I'd get that confidentiality of sources routine. Meanwhile, I'll have the cruiser swing by your place every now and then to make sure everything's okay. Make sure you don't get nervous and shoot holes in it, because it has to last a couple more years."

"Thanks."

"Oh, yeah. One thing more. I'm afraid we won't be taking any of those long guns away from your pal Tom Rimini or his girlfriend. Both of them have firearms' permits."

Really.

"Even better, the woman, Grace Shepard, has a license to carry a handgun. Seems that she feared for her life after her hubby got himself shot dead a couple of years ago, and needed to protect herself."

"She owns a handgun?"

"A 9-mm S and W, registered all nice and legal. Shoots it at a gun club pistol range. According to my sources, all confidential, you'll understand, that's where she met your friend Rimini."

"You're sure?"

"Death and taxes are sure; the rest is negotiable."

I rang off and stood there. If anyone had been looking at me they might have thought I was memorizing the shape of the telephone. But what I was really doing was trying to think clearly for a change.

22

I called Dom Agganis. The line was busy. He was probably talking with the Chief. I called Gordon R. Sullivan. His machine told me to leave a message and he'd get back to me. I told the machine what Quinn had told me and asked Sullivan to let me know if he knew anything more. I didn't have any particular reason to think that he would do it, but he might. Then I called Carla. Nobody home. She and the boys were probably all working.

I called John Skye's number. The phone there rang for quite a while before I hung up. I wasn't having much luck lately with my telephone, but not for lack of trying. AT&T would be proud of me. Maybe I should buy stock. Not willing to say die in spite of the evidence that I should, I called Rimini's cell phone.

Nothing. I realized I was very angry.

How much did I owe Tom Rimini? He'd brought bad trouble to my house, and since then he'd lied and lied and lied, and so had his girlfriend. They were armed with guns they knew how to use, and their stories were crooked as a dog's hind leg.

But if Sonny Whelen caught up with them, they were in trouble.

"I can't get through to Rimini on the phone," I said to Zee, "so I'm going out to see him. He should know that Sonny and his boys have gone missing."

"Let the police protect him!"

"I don't know what the police will do, but I do know that if I was in Rimini's place I'd want to know about Sonny dropping out of sight."

I went out into the falling light and drove to the farm. When I entered the driveway I tapped my horn a couple of times so Rimini and Grace wouldn't be taken completely by surprise. It doesn't pay to startle armed people who are already nervous.

Rimini's Honda and Grace Shepard's Explorer were parked in front of the house. Apparently Grace no longer felt the need to hide her car.

I parked beside the Honda and looked around. There was no one in sight. The front door of the house was closed and there were no lights in the windows. The loft door above the big double barn doors was slightly ajar, but the barn doors behind which Grace Shepard had hidden her Explorer earlier were closed, as were the corral gates. Everything was quiet. I knocked on the door of the house, waited, then knocked again.

"Oh, it's you," said Rimini's voice behind me.

I turned and saw him walking from the barn. Behind him, Grace was coming out of the now partially opened barn doors.

"We were wandering around looking the place over," said Rimini.

"I phoned but nobody answered. So I came over. I just got some information I think you should have."

"Sorry about the phone. We must have been out of the house. What information?"

"Sonny Whelen and some of his people have flown the coop. Nobody knows where they've gone. It's possible that they're coming here. It's possible that they're already here. I thought you should know."

Rimini came up to me and stared. "Are you sure? Who told you that?"

"A reporter friend in Boston. He has a lot of sources."

Rimini rubbed his chin and looked around. "You say some of his people are gone, too. Who? How many?"

"You know a guy called Sean? Sticks close to Sonny?"

He nodded. "Yes, I know who he is. I think he's a bodyguard."

"Well, Sean is one. Todd is another. Pete

McBride is another. McBride's buddy Bruno is another. There may be more, but those are the names I heard."

"Oh." Rimini turned as Grace Shepard came up to us. "Grace, did you hear what J.W.'s been saying? Sonny and . . ."

"I heard," said Grace. She looked at me. "Are you sure about this, Mr. Jackson?"

"I'm sure about what I heard. I can't be sure what's going on. I did think you people should have the news, for what it's worth."

She gave me a level stare. "And what do you think it is worth?"

I wondered what to make of her. "I think it's worth at least as much as that story you two told me about not knowing much about guns. What a pair of sorry liars you are."

Rimini stepped away. "What . . . ?"

The woman only smiled. "We should have told you the truth, but it seemed simpler at the time to fib. We didn't expect you to check up on us. I'm sorry."

"You're only sorry you got caught. You not only have a pistol, but you shoot at a gun club."

She made a little bow. "I underestimated your resourcefulness, Mr. Jackson. I'll not make that mistake again. Yes, it's true. I do have a pistol and I do know how to shoot it. I'm licensed to carry it, by the way, but of course you know that."

"Yes. And I know that Tom, here, met you at your gun club, which means that he's not the stranger to shooting that he pretended to be, either."

"Dear me, we have deceived you, haven't we? Yes, Tom and I can both shoot fairly well. That's why I brought the weapons down here."

"They're not just psychological props, then?"

"No, although they do work in that regard, too." She put her arm through Rimini's.

"I'm afraid I'm the nervous one," said Rimini, in a voice I had come to distrust.

"You ought to be nervous," I said. "In fact, you two should probably get out of here while the getting's good. If Whelen's coming to the island it's probably because he thinks he knows where you are."

"Or maybe where you are, Mr. Jackson," said the woman, almost flippantly.

"I'm being more careful than you are," I said, letting my irritation show. "Besides, I've no real reason to think he's after me or my family, but I know he's after Tom, and he may not like you being down here with him."

Rimini patted the woman's arm and

seemed to gather his courage. "Look," he said in a voice I thought was intended to persuade me of his moral fiber, "we appreciate everything you've done for us and we're sorry we lied about the guns, but we think this whole thing is going to work out. Until it does, we're safe here. Just give us another day or so. No one knows where we are. Even if Sonny comes looking for us, he won't find us. Please don't make us leave now. Besides, if we try to leave and if Sonny is watching the ferry lines, he'll see us."

There was something to that last argument. If Sonny had any reason to believe that Rimini and the woman planned to run, he had enough men to watch the ferry slips.

I knew I should have sent Rimini on his way the first time he'd lied to me, but my promise to Carla had stopped me before, and, in conjunction with the real threat from Whelen, it stopped me again.

"All right," I said, not liking a thing about the situation I had allowed to develop, and as angry at myself as I was at Rimini, "two more days. Then you go. One more thing: are you willing to testify against Sonny, if the authorities decide to go after him?"

He put his teeth over his lower lip, then nodded. "Yes, if it will get me out of all this."

"Okay, I'll see what I can do about getting

you into a witness protection program. You and Carla may have to move out of state and make a clean start, but considering the mess you've made for yourself in Jamaica Plain that might not be a bad thing."

He nodded again. "You're right. Do it. I'll cooperate as long as I know my family's safe."

The caring family man acted as though his mistress wasn't standing right beside him. Her face was bland, but her eyes were bright.

There was something odd about their attitudes. I stared at him. "Are you sure you haven't let it slip that you're here? That nobody knows?"

"I swear. Nobody knows."

Ananias fell down and died, but Rimini stood and gave me stare for stare.

"If you say so," I said. "I don't know what you're up to, but I'll call you if I hear anything else that you should know. I'll let the phone ring four times, then hang up and call back. If you want to hear what I have to say, pick up the second time."

I turned and walked to the Land Cruiser, feeling eyes watching me through the evening light. I was surprised to find myself experiencing the prickly fear I'd felt long ago in that far-off war when my patrol crossed openings in the forest that were excellent sites for ambush. At the truck, I paused and glanced around but saw no one other than Grace Shepard and Tom Rimini in front of the house. Maybe Rimini's nerves were having an effect on mine. I drove away and the feeling disappeared.

When I got home, Zee said, "Dom Agganis phoned. He wants you to call him back."

"What was it about?"

"He didn't say. What happened up at the farm?"

I told her. She was not happy.

"They're a pair of liars, Jeff. You can't trust them."

"I know. But they'll be gone soon."

Long ago, before my father bought it, when our house was just a hunting camp for guys who probably sat around and drank and played cards more than they actually shot at anything, somebody had put a couple of pegs over the front door where you could hang a shotgun. I had never seen a gun there before, but one was there now. My father's 12-gauge pump.

Zee's eyes followed mine. I said nothing.

"The kids can't reach it," she said in a flat voice, "but you and I can."

She was standing straight and firm. I put

my big hand on her shoulder. "Yes. Good. I'll make that call, then I'll rustle up some supper."

"It's on the stove."

"Good, again."

I called the State Police office in Oak Bluffs.

"J. W. Jackson on the box," I said in my best Brit accent when Agganis answered.

"I don't remember anybody using that phrase when I was in England," said Agganis, unimpressed.

"I've never been in England," I said, "so I'm susceptible to making errors about British usage."

"And other things."

"Zee says you called."

"I did. I had a chat with the Chief in Edgartown earlier in the day, then made a couple of calls to other people about this business of Sonny Whelen going missing. Your reporter friend has some good contacts, apparently, because what he told you was right on the money. You don't suppose he knows where Sonny's gone, do you?"

"You can ask him."

"Somebody will probably do that if they haven't already. The point is that we don't know where any of those guys you mentioned, Whelen, McBride, and the other two, are, but we're keeping our eyes open for them and I thought you might like to know that at least one familiar face has arrived on our golden shores."

"Who?"

"None other than Willard Graham, ex–DEA agent. The guy who hassled Rimini. You gave me a copy of his picture and I had some other copies printed up and spread around. One of our guys saw him drive off the boat earlier today."

"Where'd he go?"

"We don't know. You know how things are there at the five corners. Graham took a right and a truck got in front of our guy. By the time our man got to the intersection with the Edgartown road, Graham was out of sight. One choice being as good as another, our guy headed for Chilmark but never saw Graham. He could have gone anywhere."

"You get a description of the car?"

"A blue Lincoln sedan." He gave me the license number.

"Anybody else in the car?"

"A couple of people, maybe, but our man only saw Graham. He was in the suicide seat."

"When was all this?"

"About three hours ago."

Three hours. I told Agganis of my latest trip to the farm and of my conversation with Rimini and Grace Shepard. "If Graham knew where they were staying," I said, "he'd have been there when I got there, but he wasn't."

"Maybe he didn't want to be there yet," said Agganis. "Maybe he's waiting for reinforcements."

"Maybe he is."

"Your family may be the target," said Agganis.

"Thanks."

"Be careful."

"Yes."

23

I dialed the farm, let the phone ring four times, hung up and called again. Rimini answered and I told him what I'd heard.

"Graham?" His voice seemed to go away and then come back. "What's Graham doing here?"

"Maybe he's just on vacation."

The voice firmed. "I deserved that."

"Did you ever see him with anyone else?"

"No . . . no, he was always alone."

"So you don't know who else might be in that car?"

"No. I can't imagine . . ."

Was I so focused on past lies that I heard them whenever he spoke? I reminded myself that even liars tell the truth most of the time.

"Well, he's got somebody with him, so be careful."

"Thank you. We will."

Hanging up the phone, I noticed for the first time that Zee had driven two spikes into the wall above the rear door and had hung John Skye's shotgun there.

Cannons at both entrances to the house. Fort Jackson.

I went and found Zee and helped her get supper on the table.

Much later, I woke up in the dark. Zee lay curled against me, sweet and soft, one knee bent behind mine, the other thigh and calf hooked over my hip, one arm wrapped around my belly, her breath warm against my back. I listened for the sound that must have wakened me, but all I heard was the purr of a cat, Oliver Underfoot for certain, coming from the foot of the bed. Velcro, being made of sterner stuff, slept alone.

I realized instantly that it hadn't been a sound but a thought that had intruded upon my dreams: Willard Graham was not linked to Zee and me at all; he probably had never heard of us. My family wasn't threatened by him; he was on the island for some other purpose.

I didn't need the pistol I had secreted under my mattress when we went to bed; not, at least, as far as Graham and his companions were concerned.

I shut my eyes but could not shut down my thoughts. If not me, then who interested Graham? Rimini, of course. And if for no other reason than that she was there, Grace Shepard, too, fell under his sights.

But what was his intent? And who were those who accompanied him? Did they work for him, or he for them?

Was he on his own? Or did he and those with him work for or with someone? If so, who?

Sonny Whelen, perhaps?

But if he worked for Sonny, why didn't he tell Rimini that he did? But he hadn't told him. Instead, he'd told Rimini that he was a cop interested in nailing Sonny on charges of illegal gambling. But that was a lie. Graham wasn't a cop, and when he had been he'd been with the DEA, not vice. On the other hand, if he lied about being a cop, he might have been lying about everything else. Maybe he *was* working for Sonny all along, and Sonny had reasons for misleading Rimini.

Lots of ifs and maybes.

Maybe Graham worked for Pete McBride. Pete wanted Sonny's crown, and maybe Graham was sucking Rimini dry for Pete in hopes of getting some kind of an edge on Sonny. Maybe, for instance, he was going to turn everything Rimini knew over to the real cops so they'd nail Sonny and save Pete the trouble.

My maybes and ifs added up to zero.

Maybe Graham was on his own. Ex–DEA cop squeezing schoolteacher in gambling trouble. Tell me everything you know and hear, or else.

Why? I couldn't guess.

And what about Tom and Grace? They were up to something they didn't want to talk about. What?

A tangled web, indeed. Scott knew whereof he spoke; there was enough practiced deception here to go around. I had a sense of foreboding.

I slept badly and woke foggy-brained and discontented. Coffee and juice helped but did not cure my malaise. Bagels with cream cheese, lox, and red onions helped some, however, and by the time I cleaned my plate I felt almost up to par. New Yorkers are wrong about a lot of things but not about that particular meal, which is a yummer.

"You look more human than when you woke up," said Zee, gathering up her shoulder bag and giving me a kiss. "See you later."

I held her face between my hands and looked down at her. Her split lip was mending and the bruises around her eyes were fading. She looked more like her old self every day.

I kissed her and let her go, and she went off to work.

She didn't ordinarily carry that shoulder bag, and I thought I knew why she had it now. I was sure when I went to the gun cabinet and saw that her little Beretta 84F was missing. Mrs. Jackson was packing iron.

Good old Zee. The lioness was not about to let her family go unprotected, in spite of her fears that she was no longer the person she had once been. I thought of the impossibility of stepping in the same river twice, and how each of us is like that river: ever-changing, swirling atoms in endless new configurations, never quite the same persons that we were or will be, held together only by our odd sense of identity.

I washed up the breakfast dishes, stacked them in the drier beside the sink, and collected Joshua and Diana.

"Come on, kids; we're going for a drive."

"Can I steer?"

"No. You're too little."

"I'm bigger than Diana."

"But you're still not big enough. Besides, you don't have a driver's license. If a policeman caught you driving, he'd put you in jail."

"What's jail, Pa?"

"It's a room with bars on the doors and windows and no toys. They put bad people there. You wouldn't like it."

We drove up to Chilmark and I found the town clerk's office. Chilmark is the prettiest township on the Vineyard. If I didn't live in Edgartown I'd live in Chilmark if I could afford it. It's got lovely winding roads, water on three sides, the island's only official nude beach, and rolling wooded topography including the highest point on the Vineyard, a whole three-hundred-plus feet above sea level. The Quitsa end of Menemsha Pond is the prettiest site on the whole island, and at the opposite end of the pond the village of Menemsha looks like Walt Disney's idea of what a fishing village should be. All in all, it's a beautiful town with only a single flaw: no liquor store. Chilmarkers have to go to Oak Bluffs or Edgartown to get their booze.

The town clerk, like town clerks of most small towns, knew where everybody lived. There was no land registered to Willard Graham, but Howard Trucker's place was on the north side of South Road, not far from the town cemetery where faithful pilgrims still come to leave flowers, roaches, and empty beer bottles on the gravestone of John Belushi. Whether John is actually under there is widely debated, but his stone is the second most popular tourist site on the island, topped in attendance only by the Dyke Bridge on Chappaquiddick, which, decades after the accident that made it famous, still attracts the curious and the perverse. Tourists are often rather odd, but the island lives off them, so they and their money are always welcome to the Vineyard.

I paused by the entrance to Trucker's driveway. There were two mailboxes there, one with a number and the other with a name I didn't know. The clerk's directions had been explicit, so I knew I was in the right spot. I turned in. If anybody was home, I'd use the lost traveler ploy. Two kids in the car would make me more believable.

The driveway was winding and narrow and after a bit split in two. Keeping the clerk's directions in mind, I took a right. The drive climbed a rise and ended in an empty yard of uncut grass in front of a modest house with a brick chimney and a roofed front porch that extended the length of the building.

"Stay here," I said to Joshua and Diana. They nodded.

I got out and looked around. The house had that empty feeling about it that unoccupied buildings often have. I went up onto the porch and knocked on the door. While I waited, I turned and admired Howie's view. I could see Noman's Land off to the southwest and the Gay Head lighthouse up in Aquinnah. Not bad. I guessed that Howie had bought the place quite a while back, before the price of Chilmark land went through the roof. Or maybe enforcers made lots more money than I thought.

No one came to the door, so I knocked again and waited. Still nobody. I tried the door handle. Locked. If I'd brought my picks and left my children at home so they couldn't see their father breaking and entering, I could be in the house pretty quickly, but I'd brought the children and left the picks, so I was stuck outside. I peered in windows and saw that the house was as normal inside as out. I walked around to the back and tried that door. Locked. I peeked in more windows. It seemed to be an ordinary three-bedroom house. It was neat and clean. Howie might have been a strong-arm thug, but Mrs. Howie apparently was more the middle-class domestic type.

I went back to the car. Graham and his friends weren't here and never had been. They were someplace else. I hadn't narrowed the search down much. Martha's Vineyard is twenty miles long and seven miles wide, and I had eliminated exactly one house from contention. The only thing I'd learned was that Graham probably wasn't representing Howie Trucker's interests on the island. That left several million other possibilities.

"Who lives here, Pa?"

"A family named Trucker. Nobody's home."

"Why not?"

"I think their vacation's over."

I drove home, thinking.

When I passed the driveway to John Skye's farm I almost turned in, but didn't. I'd been there too often already. If I could manage it, I wouldn't go back until Rimini and the woman pulled out. Two days. I'd go back that last morning and make sure they got on their way.

At home, I called Gordon R. Sullivan, who was at his desk for a change.

"What can I do for you, J.W.?"

"You can tell me whether the minions of the law would consider putting Tom Rimini and his family in a witness protection program in exchange for testimony about Sonny Whelen's gambling operation."

"I imagine that depends on how much Mr. Rimini has to tell. The feds and the state usually protect witnesses, but if Rimini comes in and talks, we might be able to help him out."

"I get the impression that maybe I should be talking with the state guys or maybe even the feds."

I could almost see his shrug. "One thing's

for sure: they both have more money than the city does. Do you think Rimini knows anything that could nail Sonny? My impression was that he's just a little fish."

"Little tadpoles into giant oaks do grow. I don't know how much he knows, but I'd hate to see his family suffer if he talks. I think they might do just fine out in South Dakota or somewhere. They must need teachers in South Dakota."

"I wouldn't know. Tell you what I'll do. I'll ask the lieutenant so he can ask the captain so he can ask whoever it is captains ask, and when the answer gets back down to me I'll give you a call. Meanwhile, you might contact the feds and the state and see if they're interested. You'll have a better chance if Rimini actually knows something important. Does he?"

"Like I said, I don't know."

"You don't know, I don't know. I doubt if Rimini knows. I did hear one thing that might interest you."

"What's that?"

"A state cop I know says another cop told him he thinks he saw Sonny Whelen down on Cape Cod, driving toward Woods Hole."

I felt a little chill.

"When was that?"

"About three hours ago."

When I hung up I noticed that my hand was shaking just a bit. I checked the ferry schedule. It was possible that Sonny was on the island right now. If not, he could be on the noon boat. I called Dom Agganis.

24

I asked about the chances of getting Tom Rimini into a witness protection program, and Agganis said about what I expected him to say:

"That depends on what he can tell us about Sonny. If he's got enough, maybe we can do something. Have him call me and set up an appointment. I'll have somebody from the A.G.'s office listen to what he has to say."

"All right," I said, "I'll do that." Then I told him what Sullivan had said about the possible sighting on Cape Cod.

"The problem," said Agganis, "is that we don't have any reason to stop Sonny from going wherever he wants to. He hasn't done anything."

"You mean he hasn't done anything that you can prove."

"That's what I mean. Sonny is just another citizen until we can begin to make some dirt stick to him. If he wants to take a Vineyard holiday, there's nobody to say he can't."

"Well, don't you think it's just a little bit

odd that Sonny and Graham and several other Boston area guys probably in Sonny's gang are all showing up here on the Vineyard at the same time, just when Tom Rimini and Grace Shepard happen to be hiding out from Sonny?"

"Maybe the Mafia is going to have another big Appalachian Convention–type meeting, only this time on the Vineyard. I mean even the evil empire likes to convene in a nice vacation place, just like the AMA. Anyway, we'll have some people at the docks when the next boats come in. In fact, we'll have more than one somebody this time, so we won't lose Sonny like we lost Graham. We can probably trail him, but we can't arrest him until he does something illegal, and Sonny never does any illegal thing himself unless it's very personal."

"If he's got the hots for Grace Shepard, he might take it personally that she's shacked up with Tom Rimini."

"He might at that, especially since one theory is that Sonny had Ralph Shepard hit so he could get at Grace. But that's only conjecture, of course."

"My impression is that Sonny doesn't leave Charlestown all that often. If he's come down here, it's for a reason."

"Brilliant, Watson. And people say that

you're just a brainless schmuck."

"I want you to write this down and credit it to me, Dom. Ready? 'Something is rotten in the state of Denmark.' Got that?"

"Go eat some lunch and leave me alone."

I did that, feeding myself and my offspring slabs of homemade bread slathered with butter and honey. Delish!

Then I mowed the lawn with the mower I'd salvaged from the dump years before. All it needed was a cleaned carburetor and a new starter cord and it was just fine. People throw away a lot of perfectly good stuff.

Mowing grass is a mindless operation, so you can think of other things while you do it. I thought about all of the shady people who were casting shadows on the island. The pattern they composed was elusive, but one thing seemed clear: Tom Rimini was at the center of it somehow.

I tried to remember everything I had seen, heard, or been told, known lies and all. I tried to figure which things I'd presumed were true might also be lies.

I started with Howie Trucker. He'd told me that day from his hospital bed that Sonny had sent him and Logan after Tom Rimini, but he didn't know why. I believed him because Howie had believed I'd kill him if he lied. Then, at the Green Harp, Sonny had indirectly admitted that sending Logan and Trucker had been a mistake, because Logan couldn't keep his hands off pretty women. He'd said that Logan and Trucker had only been given the job because they were already on the island, vacationing. He hadn't said why Rimini was being sought, but what he had said had backed up Howie's story.

Rimini had told me that he'd fled to the island because of his gambling addiction and because Sonny had found out about his connection with Graham, who wanted to know everything Rimini could tell him about Sonny and his numbers games. Carla had told me the same thing. They agreed that Carla had sent Rimini to my house and that later Carla had been frightened into telling that to Sonny's thugs.

So far, so good. But now things got less clear: Graham wasn't a cop anymore when he'd contacted Rimini; he was an ex-agent for the DEA, which dealt with drugs, not gambling. So he'd lied to Rimini about who he was and what he was up to.

Then Pete McBride and his muscle, Bruno, had trailed me out to Carla's house. Were they working for Sonny or for themselves? Pete was nominally one of Sonny's gang, but had the reputation of wanting

Sonny's job. I didn't know why Sonny hadn't already hit him just to be on the safe side, but he hadn't. Maybe because he wasn't sure if the rumors were true. In any case, McBride might be Sonny's man or he might be just the opposite.

Meanwhile, back on the ranch, Tom Rimini had lied about almost everything. Grace had done the same, but with more panache. And they had a little armory that both knew how to use. They said they had a plan, but didn't say what it was, and said that they only needed to hide out a couple more days. It was quite possible that they were just telling more lies, of course, but in any case I planned to move them off John Skye's place when their two days were up. I'd had enough of Tom Rimini.

What about Carla? I'd been drawn to her first by a sense of duty, then by feelings and a physical attraction I thought I'd gotten past long ago, and I had believed everything she'd told me. But now, in the midst of lies and mysteries, I wondered if I'd been wrong.

I could see her face, and my lips and arms remembered her warmth. If she had deceived me, it wouldn't be the first time a woman made a man into a fool. But I'd been married to her for five years, and in that time had never known her to be cruel, not even when she was leaving me, and I hadn't seen any changes in her when we met in Jamaica Plain. No, I'd put my money on Carla's honesty, win or lose.

It was a relief to believe her, but a sorrow to realize that I could not save her from the pain that would come to her when she finally knew the truth about the husband who was wronging her.

Which meant that I actually owed little or nothing at all to Tom Rimini, since saving him would not stop the hurt that was coming to Carla.

I finished the mowing, cleaned off the mower and put it away, then washed up and had a Sam Adams. The beer was dark and cool and just what I needed.

I considered everything again, then had a small thought that should have occurred to me before: Tom Rimini had lied about Grace Shepard, and both he and Grace had lied first about the guns, and then about their knowledge of how to use them. If they lied about those things, what else might they have lied about?

How about everything? Rimini and Carla had told me, for example, that Sonny was after him because of Tom's gambling debts and his contact with Graham. But Carla knew nothing firsthand about Tom's gambling and had never even seen Graham. All she knew or thought she knew was what Tom had told her, and Tom might have been lying to her, too.

What if Graham had never hassled Tom at all and had never claimed to be a cop? What if they had been meeting for some other reason?

What reason?

I had to be careful not to get too Byzantine in my thinking. Things were complicated enough without me imagining them to be even worse.

I called Quinn. "You're getting to be my best customer," he said.

"There may be a story for you down here on the island."

"My ears are up. Even if there isn't a story, an excuse to visit the Blessed Isle is always welcome. What story?"

I told him of the arrival of the Boston players. "I don't know what it's all about, yet, but the cast of characters is interesting."

"Indeed. Your guest room available?"

"Sure, but first you can do something for me."

He groaned. "What?"

"Check back and tell me everything you can about a drug dealer named Ralph

Shepard. He was chief supplier in Jamaica Plain until he got himself shot to death a couple of years ago. I want to know what kind of a guy he was. Was he laid-back and trusting? Was he nervous and scared? Was he sweet? Was he sour? Did he extend credit? Mostly, I want to know if he was the kind of guy who'd let a stranger into his car, because somebody sitting in the shotgun seat put a hole in his head. Can you do that? If you can, do it and call me back."

"I can do it," said Quinn. "Go make the bed in the guest room."

An hour later he called back. "I'm on my way down. Tell Zee and watch her face light up. A real man is on his way."

"What about Ralph Shepard?"

"Ralph was the nervous type, as well he should be, considering his trade. He was smart and he didn't trust people much, so he kept a layer of small-time dealers between him and his real customers. If he relaxed anywhere, it was at home. The only person he'd have let into his car was somebody he knew and trusted, the more fool he."

It is a truism that we tend to get murdered by people we know and trust. Family members and friends kill each other every day.

"They find the weapon?"

"Nope."

"One theory is that Sonny waxed him so he could get at his wife."

"Sonny is slick, so maybe he arranged the hit. But Ralph knew that Sonny had an eye on his wife, so I don't see him letting anybody dangerous into his car."

"Maybe Sonny got to one of the dealers working for Shepard, and the dealer did the job."

"The police rounded up Ralph's retailers, but never got anywhere. The dealers were small-fry, and any time they'd done was for nonviolent stuff. Possession with intent to sell, and that sort of thing. Most of them were just supporting their own habits. The cops never really had a solid suspect. No more time to gossip, I'm heading for the island. Set an extra plate on the table!"

I got a container of chowder out of the freezer and set it to thaw, then I called John Skye's house using the same code as before. Rimini picked up the receiver. I told him about Agganis's offer to talk with him about the possibility of getting into the witness protection program.

"It's the best I can do for you," I said. "Maybe you and Carla can go out West someplace where they need teachers and leave all this behind you."

Rimini seemed appropriately grateful.

"That sounds good, J.W. Thanks. I'll think about it, I really will. It might be the best solution."

Sure. He and Carla and Grace would find happiness together out in the golden West.

"Do what you think is best," I said, and rang off. I had done my duty as far as Tom Rimini was concerned, and it was a freeing experience.

Less liberating was a confused scenario that was forming in my brain. I could think of two people who could have gotten into that car with Ralph Shepard and both of them were on the island. I also thought I knew where Sonny Whelen would establish his headquarters if he arrived as well. The game was afoot.

25

Whelen's, Rimini's, and Graham's groups were all converging, and it was beyond belief that there was no tie among them or that the center of the knot was Rimini. It was not hard to believe that Rimini had somehow revealed his whereabouts to both Graham and Whelen, for he seemed to be set on talking to people on the mainland. I knew he'd talked with Grace Shepard and Carla, and he might well have telephoned someone else. And anyone he spoke to might have told what he or she knew to someone else, deliberately or by accident or from fear. It was possible, even probable, then, that Graham or Whelen or both knew Rimini was hiding out on John Skye's farm. And even if they might not know exactly where the farm was, they probably knew it was in Edgartown and wouldn't be too long in finding it.

And then what?

I could guess what Whelen had in mind. His reputation for participating in matters that were personal to him suggested that he had come to deal with Tom or Grace or both of them. That did not bode well for Tom and Grace.

Less guessable was the relationship among Graham, Rimini, and Whelen. If Graham was working for Whelen, why hadn't they come down together? Or, if circumstance obligated them to come separately, why wasn't Graham waiting for Whelen to show up at Howie Trucker's house?

For that was where I expected Whelen to make his headquarters while he organized his forces. Sonny could afford to stay anywhere he wanted to, of course, but being in a profession that eschewed close attention, he probably preferred to be as inconspicuous as possible. Trucker's house was ideal for his purposes, as Sonny knew from past visits. It was an unobtrusive middle-class dwelling that was set well off the road at the end of an inconspicuous driveway, and thus offered both security and privacy. What more could a guy like Sonny desire?

But if Graham was working for or with Sonny, why hadn't he been at the house, waiting for him, when I'd driven in? He would have known when Sonny was coming and he had to wait somewhere, and that was the logical place.

But he hadn't been there.

Curiouser and curiouser.

Or maybe not.

What if Graham didn't work for or with Sonny? I had no more reason, after all, to think that he did than to think that he didn't. If Graham wasn't Sonny's man, then what was he up to? He wasn't Rimini's pal, for sure, not after the hard time he'd given Tom.

But wait. What if Graham and Tom were thick? What if Graham was Tom's ally instead of his enemy?

It was as though a switch had been thrown in my brain. Gears began to creak into motion after long inactivity. I oiled them with speculation. They moved more smoothly.

If Tom and Graham were pals, it was possible that their relationship had never been about money, but about drugs, since that was Graham's area of expertise. Maybe Tom wasn't in the gambling business but in the drug business. Or, more likely, he was in both. Sonny Whelen was in both, too, and wanted to get back into the Jamaica Plain trade. Nervous but crafty Ralph Shepard had run the drug trade there, but Whelen had been thwarted when Ralph had got himself hit, because somebody else had moved faster than Sonny and had taken over Ralph's trade. Who? I didn't know. How about the guy who had hit Ralph? Who might that be?

How about Willard Graham?

How *about* Willard Graham. He had the expertise and the experience and the contacts. All he had to do was kill Ralph, and he'd be in the driver's seat.

But Ralph would never let anybody he didn't know into his car.

Unless the guy had a badge. If Graham no longer had his old shield, he sure knew where to get one that looked real. And Graham had the further advantage of looking and acting like a cop because that's what he'd been. A corrupt cop, admittedly, but a cop nevertheless, and any perp can tell you that most cops smell like cops before they ever show their shields. Hell, even I was still mistaken for the law sometimes, and I hadn't been in uniform for fifteen years.

So nervous Ralph might have let Graham into his car because he didn't want trouble with a narc.

On the other hand, if he saw Graham or any other guy who looked like a cop coming close, he'd probably just have put the pedal to the metal and gotten out of there in the time-honored way of avoiding trouble with the fuzz.

So maybe Graham hadn't hit Ralph, although he remained on the short list. If not Graham, then who?

Grace.

Ralph might be too nervous to let Graham into his car, but he would have welcomed his wife. In fact, she was probably the one person he never would have expected to kill him. After all, they were married and lived together, and she'd never killed him yet although she no doubt had had plenty of chances, just as all wives have.

But why would she have done it?

A fit of pique? Maybe. People killed in bursts of rage, often ruing the act the moment it was done.

But Grace hadn't struck me as the burst-of-rage type. She was nothing if not cool. If she killed her husband, it wasn't because of uncontrollable anger.

Why, then? Perhaps because he stood between her and something she wanted.

What? Not money, supposedly, because he was making good money and they were living well, as suggested by her almost new Explorer.

Another man?

Tom Rimini?

Why not? Tom was bored with his wife, and Grace was bored with her husband. They had met at the gun club and hit it off. One thing leads to another. If Carla gets wise, all she can do is get a divorce, but unlike Carla, Ralph carries a gun, so Grace and

Tom can't afford to have him catch them while they cavort. Fortunately for them, Ralph is in a profession where sudden death is not an unexpected event. So one night Ralph is parked in his usual spot and who is he surprised to see but Grace. She smiles and waves and gets into the car.

"What are you doing here, sweetie?" he asks, probably not too happy to have her there on the street where he's working.

"This," she says, and shoots him in the head.

Then she gets out and walks away into the dark.

She gets the apartment, the Explorer, the insurance, and Tom Rimini. Not bad. I could see it happening.

She also gets more attention from Sonny Whelen. They play around and Sonny is serious about her. That means he doesn't like having Tom Rimini sharing Grace's bed. Tom keeps it up and Sonny gets more put out. He sends his people after Tom, and Carla, having been fed a line about Tom's gambling problem, sends her husband to the first safe place she can think of: my house. But Sonny's thugs pressure Carla and she talks, so Sonny phones Logan and Trucker, who are already on the island, and has them go get Tom. But they find Zee instead of Tom and the rest is history. Now Sonny is really pissed, and when he learns where Tom is, he comes after him in person.

How did he learn? From blabby Tom? Maybe, but maybe not.

Anyway, that explains Tom and Grace and Sonny being here, but it doesn't explain Graham.

"Pa."

"What?"

"Diana can't throw straight. You come and throw."

"He's mean, Pa, he won't let me play!"

"You two see that sign there above the door?"

"Yes, Pa."

"What does it say?"

Diana stared at the sign, then shook her head. "I don't know, Pa. I can't read."

Joshua sounded the letters: "N . . . O . . . S . . . N . . . I . . . V . . . E . . . L . . . I . . . N . . . G."

"That's right. It says NO SNIVELING. That means we don't snivel in this house. Unless we absolutely have to, that is."

Diana's mouth and eyes turned down. "But I have to, Pa. Josh won't let me play. He's mean."

"He's not mean. He just wants somebody who can catch the ball and throw it back. Come on. I'll go outside with you and the

277

three of us will play. Josh can throw it to me and I'll throw it to you and then you throw it to me and I'll throw it to Josh."

So we did that, because I didn't care if Diana caught it or threw it straight and because Joshua, in spite of his big brother airs, wasn't much better. For that matter, I never had a shot at the big leagues, either. Together, we tossed, caught, dropped, and chased the ball under the summer sun. While we did, I brooded about Graham.

He was here and he was not alone. Who was with him? What did they all want?

Something having to do with Rimini, but what?

Drugs.

Rimini was hot for the wife, later the widow, of Jamaica Plain's prime supplier. If I thought that Ralph would let Tom get into Ralph's car and if I thought that Tom had the backbone to do it, I'd have thought that Tom might have hit Ralph because of Grace. But I didn't think either of those possibilities was likely. Still, that didn't mean that Tom wasn't involved. Tom was smart and dishonest, a hazardous combination, and ambition would make him even more dangerous.

Suppose Rimini's interests and Graham's interests were linked. Suppose Rimini wanted the woman, Grace wanted Rimini, and Graham wanted to control the drug supply in Jamaica Plain. With Ralph gone, all of them got what they wanted. *Voilà!* Just like that.

A nice partnership, indeed. Maybe Grace and Tom were satisfied with just each other, but on the other hand maybe Graham shared some of his newly acquired drug money with them. Why not? Together they'd gotten rid of Ralph, so together they would apportion the rewards. Good friends sharing good times.

On the ocean of my thought, something was hull down on the horizon. I could see its topmasts but the rest of it was out of sight. It made me curious and uneasy. It was something I should be able to bring into view, but could not.

Back to the Graham/Rimini thesis.

If Graham was Rimini's friend and partner, it made him Whelen's enemy. If that were the case, then Graham wouldn't be waiting for Whelen at Howie Trucker's house, but would more likely be visiting Rimini at John Skye's farm.

Why?

Not to enjoy a Vineyard vacation with his pals, certainly. Something else.

The ship beyond the horizon sailed into

view. It came closer and I clapped a telescope to my mind's eye. The ship had a blue hull and was named *Abraham Lincoln*, and when I saw her I suddenly knew what was going on.

26

It was a bloody scenario, if I was right, and there wasn't much time for me to verify my suspicions or to do anything about them.

"Pa, get the ball!"

"You kids play together for a few minutes."

I went into the house and phoned Helen Fonseca.

"You're here more than my husband is," she said. "Sure, bring the kids down."

"Thanks. It'll be the last time for a while."

"Nonsense. I love having them around. Keeps me young."

"Me, too, but I need a couple of hours without them."

I cleaned up the kids, grabbed a phone book, and drove to Helen's house. Josh and Diana were glad to go, having fond memories of her cookies and milk and her willingness to spoil them.

"I'll be back," I said to her. "I'm going up-island to Howie Trucker's house."

"Howie Trucker? I don't think I know him."

"He works out of Boston. Some of his

business associates are staying up there and they need to talk with me."

That was true, although they didn't know it.

I drove up the West Tisbury Road. A half mile past John Skye's driveway I pulled off to the side and parked. I got my field glasses, stuck my old .38 under my shirt, and went into the woods. After a while I could see John's south pasture in front of me. When he and his family were there, the twins' horses ran in that pasture. Now, the Skyes were out West and their horses were being boarded on a farm up-island.

There was a stand of scrub oak and trees along the edge of the pasture leading up to the back of the barn and the corrals. I put the glasses on the yard and house. Rimini's green Honda was parked in its usual spot and beside it was the Ford Explorer.

No people were in sight. I watched for a while and saw no one come out or go into the house. Then I moved back into the woods and worked my way toward the barn, pausing now and then to study it through the glasses. No eyes seemed to be upon me. I made it to a small storage shed, took a final peek around a corner, saw no one, and sprinted across a small corral to the back of the barn.

I knew John and Mattie's place well, having cared for it for years. There was a back door leading into the tack room, and I went to it and listened. No sounds. I eased the door open and slipped inside. The tack room smelled of oil and leather. There was harness on the walls and there were saddles and blankets and tools in their places. I crossed to another door and listened again. Nothing. I opened the door a crack and peeked through.

There, where Grace Shepard's Explorer had once been secreted, was a blue Lincoln sedan.

A ladder to the loft was to the right of the car. I waited and listened, then cat-footed across to the front of the barn. I put an eye to the crack between the big double doors. The yard between the house and barn was empty. I turned back and went up the ladder.

There was still some baled hay in the loft, left over from last summer. I went to the loft door. There was a narrow mattress on the floor a yard back from the door. The door was slightly ajar, just as it had been when last I'd looked at it. Now I saw why: a new hook and eye held it that way. I looked through the opening and had a perfect view of the yard and the front of the house. I remembered the uneasy feeling I'd had when I'd last been down in that yard and now knew why I'd had it. Someone had been watching me from this very spot. Possibly over the sights of a rifle.

Suddenly the door of the house opened and Rimini and a man I recognized as Graham came out and walked toward the barn. I didn't hesitate, but trotted back to the ladder, climbed down, and went back out through the tack room. When I thought the two men were near the front of the barn, I sprinted across the yard to the shed, then, ducking, moved away through the scrub oak and trees until I was well out of sight. There I turned and put the glasses on the barn. No one. I turned and walked through the woods until I reached the Land Cruiser.

I was sweating and my hands were shaking, but I didn't have time for a case of nerves. I started the truck and drove to West Tisbury, then took South Road to Chilmark. When I got to Howie Trucker's driveway I stopped, put the .38 under the seat, then found Howie's telephone number and dialed it on the cell phone.

A voice I didn't recognize said, "Yeah?"

"This is J. W. Jackson. Tell Sonny that I'm coming up to the house in an old Toyota Land Cruiser. I have something to tell him,

I'm alone, and I won't be armed."

"What . . . ?"

But I'd rung off before he could finish the question. I put the phone away and turned up the driveway. I felt almost ethereal. I saw no one until I reached the grassy yard in front of the house, then I saw two men on the porch. One of them was Todd, and the other was the man who'd patted me down in the rest room of the Green Harp. Todd's hands were behind his back.

I got out of the truck, spread my arms, and walked toward them.

"That's far enough," said Todd.

I stopped and the other man came off the porch. "Just stand still, Mr. Jackson." I did and he patted me down just as thoroughly as he had done before. "I see you still have that pocketknife, Mr. Jackson. Just leave it be. You can put down your hands."

I did that.

"Go inside, Mr. Jackson."

I went up the stairs and into the house. Todd came after me. Sonny Whelen was in the living room.

"So we meet again," he said. "The last time it was on my ground. This time it's on yours, more or less. What was it you wanted to tell me, Mr. Jackson?"

He didn't offer me a chair, so I stood.

"You're walking into an ambush," I said. "You think that you're going to surprise and nail Tom Rimini, but it's a setup."

Behind me, Todd made a primitive sound. Whelen studied me.

"I don't know what you're talking about," he said.

"I'm talking about you and your men going to the place where Rimini is staying, thinking that you've got the element of surprise and the guns, and probably thinking that Rimini is a wimp to boot. I don't know how you found out where he is, but I wouldn't be surprised if it was a call from Grace Shepard with some tale about needing to be saved from Tom Rimini's clutches."

His pale eyes hardened. "You're an imaginative man," he said. "Go on."

"You know your reasons for coming here better than I do, but I'd guess they have a lot to do with the woman. I'd guess that you don't like her being down here with Rimini."

"You keep her name out of your fucking mouth!"

White fire blazed in those eyes.

Fear ran up and down my spine, but I only nodded. "That'll be hard to do, but I'll try. I don't really know or care why you came, but

I want no more bloodshed here where I live, and I can tell you for sure that if you go charging in after Rimini you won't come out alive."

His lip curled. "You know that, do you? Todd, here, is an army in himself. And Sean only looks mild and sweet. I don't think we have to worry about a womanizing schoolteacher."

I kept my voice level. "You may need more than two one-man armies. Your womanizing schoolteacher is an expert rifleman, and he's got an army of his own waiting for you: an ex–DEA agent named Willard Graham, your old pal Pete McBride, and that thug of his, Bruno. And there's a pistol-packing woman who brought Rimini a shotgun and a 30.06 when she moved in with him. Maybe that's not enough firepower to make you careful, but it would be enough for me."

Whelen studied me. "You told me once you didn't know where Rimini was. That was a lie. Maybe you're lying again."

"When we talked before, I thought Rimini was just a small-time gambler who deserved a break. If I still thought that, I wouldn't be here."

"If this bum lied once, he'll lie twice," said Todd. "Let me have him."

Whelen ignored him. "How do you know all this you're telling me? Why should I believe you? Maybe you're working with them."

"Yeah," said Todd.

"A cop saw Graham come off the ferry in a blue Lincoln. I saw McBride in a car like that when I was talking with Rimini's wife just after I talked with you. Two and two equals four. I didn't know whether McBride was working for you or for Rimini or for himself, but just now I scouted the farm where Rimini's staying. Rimini's car and the woman's Explorer are parked in front of the house, right where you'd expect them to be. But the Lincoln is in the barn, out of sight. Upstairs in the loft, a door has been fastened open just a crack. There's a mattress on the floor just inside the door. A man with a rifle can lie there and have a clean shot at anybody in the yard or in front of the house. That's where you and your two-man army would park if you were after Rimini."

Ice replaced the fire in Whelen's eyes. I went on.

"I figure that you've been suckered, Sonny. When you and Todd and Sean climb out of your car, you won't take ten steps before the three of you are Swiss cheese. And then Rimini and the others will all plead self-defense, because the cops will find your corpses with guns in your hands. You'll be dead and the shooters will all walk, and . . ." I paused.

"And what?"

"And Pete McBride will finally get to take over in Charlestown. Graham will work with him and keep on supplying narcotics in Jamaica Plain, Rimini will get the woman and a chair at Pete's right hand, and everybody will live happily ever after. I think they've been planning this for a while. It was going to happen somewhere, but then Rimini ran to my place and I put him in a safe house that was perfect for them. All they had to do was get you to come down, and that wasn't too hard because you like to handle personal matters yourself. You're famous for it."

"Why that bitch," said Whelen, almost to himself. "She set me up." He thought for a while, then looked at me. "You know a problem I got? I got nobody to tell me when I'm being stupid. Nobody wants to tell me something they don't think I want to hear. Ain't that right, Todd?"

"It ain't for me to tell you anything, Sonny."

"That's what I mean," said Whelen. "I read somewhere once that every king needs a fool to keep him from being a fool himself. I got no fool. Somebody should have told me about Grace, Todd."

"You weren't gonna get it from me, boss."

"Would you have believed it if somebody'd told you?" I asked.

He shook his head. "Probably not." Then he eyed me again. "I still don't get why you're talking to me about all this. We're not what you'd call friends. Especially not after Logan being stupid like he was."

"It's simple enough. This is a nice, quiet island most of the time. I want it to get that way again and stay that way. I don't want any gangland massacres here, and I especially don't want one on the farm where Rimini is staying. That farm belongs to a friend of mine, and when he comes back later this summer, I don't want him to find the house full of bullet holes and wrapped in yellow tape. Tomorrow I'll be going down there and moving Rimini out. I'll get help from the cops, if I need to, but he'll be leaving the island one way or another. After that, none of this is my problem."

The corner of Whelen's lip curled up. "You don't care who gets killed as long as it doesn't happen on Martha's Vineyard."

I thought of Carla and her sons and of the sorrow they would bear if Tom Rimini died.

"I care," I said, "but a long time ago I decided I was tired of trying to make the world a perfect place. I came down here to be a fisherman and to live a quiet life. You and your kind have made my wife a killer and given me bad dreams, so I want you and all the other people in this sorry affair to finish your business some other place. The farther away, the better."

"Watch your mouth," said Todd.

"If we go into the farm the way you went in, we can turn that ambush around," said Whelen.

"I don't want that," I said.

"Shut up," said Todd. "Who the fuck cares what you want?"

My mouth was dry as Death Valley. "If you go down there, I'll be going to the cops."

Sonny's voice got very cold. "Dead men tell no tales," he said.

"You owe me this," I said. "Your boys Logan and Trucker did my wife and daughter wrong."

"And paid for it."

"And I just saved your life. You take your war off island and we're square."

Behind me, I heard a sound that might have been that of a pistol being cocked.

"Hold it, Todd," said Whelen. He stared

at me. "You're a hard case, Mr. Jackson."

"No, I'm just a man who likes peace and quiet."

He nodded. "You go home now, Mr. Jackson. I'll keep in mind what you've just said. Todd, show Mr. Jackson to the door and tell Sean to come in here. Good-bye, Mr. Jackson. Nice talking with you."

I turned and went out the door, walking on legs that felt like melting ice.

27

As I drove back to Edgartown, I found myself having contradictory thoughts about Carla. She deserved a better man than the lying, adulterous, murderous Tom I thought I knew; but on the other hand, maybe she didn't know that man at all, but knew, instead, a Tom unknown to me, a quiet schoolteacher Tom, who, in spite of his weakness for gambling, could give her the stable and secure life that she'd never felt she had when she'd been married to me.

You could never tell how people saw each other or how they needed each other. Both women and men loved people that no one else on earth would even want to know. And no matter how rotten those people might seem to be to others, to their lovers they were more valuable than heaven itself.

Humans are strange creatures. We can love murderers and stone saints, all in the same day.

I'm probably no exception.

I stopped in front of the field of dancing statues in West Tisbury and called John Skye's house, using the code I'd agreed upon with Tom Rimini. When he answered, I told him where I was and that I was coming by to see him. He was protesting when I hung up.

I drove slowly toward Edgartown to give him and his cohorts time to figure out where to hide and how to handle me. I could already feel the crosshairs on my neck.

When I drove in, I found Rimini's car and the Ford Explorer in front of the house, right where I'd seen them from the barn. A glance revealed that the loft door was still ajar; then, as I got out of the Toyota, Rimini and Grace Shepard stepped out onto the front porch. The woman's face was a mask, but Rimini was trying a smile. I felt like a target on a missile range.

The woman spoke first. "How do you do, Mr. Jackson? What brings you here?"

"I want to talk to Tom," I said. "In private."

"We have no secrets," she said with a smile I wouldn't have believed in a thousand years.

"Afterward, he can tell you any part of it he likes," I said. I hooked a finger at him. "Let's talk."

He gave her a fast look, then flicked his eyes at the barn, then brought them back to me.

"We're together," he said, brushing those nervous hands of his together. "Anything you say to me, you can say to her."

"Maybe you're right," I said, letting my irritation show. "Maybe she shouldn't trust you. But what I have to say, I'll only say to you. After that, you can do what you want with it."

The hands rubbed together. He took a breath. He gave her a furtive glance. She stared at me with animal eyes. Nobody said anything.

"All right," I said, "fuck you." I turned back to the truck.

He heard the anger in my voice. "Wait," he said. "Okay, let's talk."

I walked to the far side of the yard and he followed me. The woman stood on the porch and watched us.

"What is it, J.W.?"

My voice was flat, but he paled as he heard it. I said, "This is what it is, Tom. Sonny Whelen knows about the rifle in the barn and the shotgun in the house. He knows about Graham and Pete McBride and Bruno being here, and he knows about Grace and you and the ambush you've set up, so he won't be coming to see you here."

His voice was tremulous. "What are you talking about? What are you saying?" Then, almost in a whisper. "How could he know?"

It gave me pleasure, I must admit. I put my head close to his. "Because I told him, Tom."

He looked at me with horror but, curiously, not with doubt. "How? How could you . . . ?"

I ignored his questions. "The important thing is that there'll be no ambuscade here today. Sonny is going home. Later he'll decide what's going to happen to who and when it'll happen. Your ass and your pals' asses are in the frying pan, Tom. Your game is over."

Fear made his eyes bright. "Jesus!"

"For once you're going to do what you said you're going to do," I said. "You're going to leave the island tomorrow, and you're going to take your gang of assassins with you. I'll be by in the morning and if you're not gone, I'll bring in the cops. I'll have all of you in the Dukes County jail on charges of conspiracy to commit murder. And I may even be able to make it stick."

"Jesus," he said again. He looked faint. It turned my stomach, but I made myself go on:

"If you really have enough dirt to nail Sonny, you may be able to make a deal with the cops and get into the witness protection program. If you do or if you don't, I advise you to get out of this territory and try to make a life someplace where Sonny can't find you. I think that your wife and boys will probably join you when they can. Carla loves you, for reasons that escape me. She can sell the house, and the two of you can probably get jobs out West someplace where they need schoolteachers. Sonny isn't so crazy that he'll waste a lot of money tracking down a little shit like you. You aren't worth it." I looked at Grace Shepard, who was watching us. "On the other hand, if you hang around Boston, I wouldn't give two cents for your chances. Sonny didn't get where he is by putting up with local scum. Do what you want."

"Why are you telling me all this?"

I knew why. "Because your wife loves you and she deserves more than she's gotten from you so far. You're a lying, two-timing, would-be murderer, but you haven't actually done much that will put you in jail. Gambling debts aren't illegal in this state, and as far as I know you haven't killed anybody yet, although this bungled try might have changed that. If you shake Grace and go someplace far from Boston and straighten your life out, there's a chance you can give Carla and your boys a decent life.

On the other hand, you're such a fuckup that you'll probably let Sonny blow you away. And that wouldn't be such a loss that Carla and the boys couldn't get over it. It's your call."

I left him and walked to the Toyota, got in, and drove away. In my rearview mirror I watched him look after me, then start back toward the house. I thought I saw a flicker of movement behind the loft door, but that might have been my imagination.

I was home, stirring the pot of chowder, when Quinn phoned from Vineyard Haven.

"Just got in. Send Zee to get me. We need to be alone."

I conveyed the message and Zee laughed. "I'll go pick him up. Poor man; he needs a woman of his own."

"He's got plenty of women," I said, "but none of them belong just to him. I think he likes it that way."

"He just hasn't met the right one, yet."

"He's met you."

"But I'm taken. See you in a bit."

She went off in her little Jeep.

"Pa?"

"What is it, Josh?"

"Have you ever been in Greece?"

"No, but someday I'd like to go there."

"I want to make a Parthenon. Ma showed

me a picture of it. She said it's in Greece, then we found Greece on the globe."

Some children want to color pictures of Mickey Mouse. Mine wanted to build a Parthenon.

"Will you need any help, Josh?"

"Yeah, Pa. Will you help me?"

"Me, too," said Diana. "I want to help, too."

"You're too little," said Joshua, stepping closer and putting a possessive arm around a paternal leg.

"We're going to need all the help we can get," I said. "It's not easy to build a Parthenon." I stirred my chowder and tasted it. Just a wee bit more salt. I added it, stirred, and tasted again. Better. Maybe some Bean Supreme to give it that little something more. I eyeballed the proper dosage, stirred, and tasted again. Yes. I put the pot on a back burner and turned the heat very low.

"Let's look at the picture, Josh."

We went into the living room and opened the book on the coffee table. The loveliest of ruins lay before our eyes.

"The roof blew up," said Josh. "They had a war and some guys had gunpowder stored in it and it blew up."

"It's made out of rock," I said. "Maybe we could make one out of wood."

"We've got wood, Pa."

True. I had a pile of wood scraps left over from when I'd built the kids' bedrooms a while back. I'd been using it for fireplace kindling, but there was enough to build a Parthenon, too, as long as it wasn't too big.

By the time Zee and Quinn arrived, our Parthenon plans had shrunk down to model size and our building was going to be made of wood scraps painted white. Our acropolis would be the mound of dirt left over when I dug the pond for the goldfish. The pond would be our Aegean Sea, and our Parthenon would overlook it from on high.

"This is how small jobs turn into big ones," said Quinn. "You start out building a Parthenon and you end up having to build an Aegean Sea and an acropolis before you can even begin your temple."

"We'll get it done," I said. "Athens wasn't built in a day. In fact, you can help. Tomorrow, instead of going fishing, you can have a shovel and help dig the pond."

"Hoo ha!" said Quinn. "That'll be the day! Point me at your vodka, Zeolinda, my sweet. I'm in a state of shock and I need a drink to quiet my nerves. You'll join me, of course, while these three slave over their blueprints."

"But of course," said Zee. "Follow me."

"Anywhere."

They went into the kitchen.

"We're going to have goldfish?" asked Diana.

"Yes."

She thought a moment. Then, "Can we have a dog, too?"

But I was ready. "No. No dogs. Just goldfish."

Quinn and Zee came out of the kitchen carrying trays of drinks, crackers, cheese, and smoked bluefish pâté.

"We have enough for three," said Zee.

"Against my advice," said Quinn.

"It's big-people time on the balcony," I said to Josh and Diana.

"Okay, Pa. Can we start the Parthenon tomorrow?"

"I hope so."

I went up and they went out into the yard so they could keep an eye on their elders.

I sat down and took a sip of icy Luksusowa. Delish! I tried some crackers loaded with cheese and pâté. Double delish!

"Okay," said Quinn. "Now tell me about this Pulitzer Prize-winning story I'm down here to write."

"There may not be any story," I said.

"What!?"

"You're the newsman," I said. "Listen to my tale, then decide for yourself."

I told him about my week, and about this day in particular. When I was done, we all sat there and looked out over Nantucket Sound, where the evening boats were coming in to harbor. It was a peaceful scene, with slanting western light casting our shadows over the gardens below, and a soft wind whispering through the trees. In the yard, Joshua and Diana played with the cats. There wasn't a murderer in sight.

"I can make a short but good nonstory out of it," said Quinn. "Mysterious gangster gatherings on Beautiful Martha's Vineyard, and like that. People will wonder what it was all about, and I'll drop a few hints without really saying anything." He turned to Zee. "On the other hand, a personal interview with you could do wonders for my career. Better yet, I can write it so nobody else will feel they have to talk with you themselves. I can send the wolves away to other hunting grounds and get your story out at the same time. What do you say?"

"I've been thinking about that possibility," said Zee. "I wish there wasn't any story, but since there is, you can have it."

"There," I said to Quinn. "Now aren't you glad you came down?"

"Damned right. While you're digging your pond, Zee can take me fishing, and while we're hauling them in on Wasque she can tell me her tale. And I'll use my expense account to buy the champagne we'll share on the beach."

I joined the laugh, but even as I did, some part of me was listening for sirens headed toward John Skye's farm and wondering if nearer neighbors had heard the sound of gunfire there. Gangsters have changed their plans before, after all. The vision in my brain was not a pretty one.

28

Zee wasn't working the next day, so after breakfast, while she stayed with the cubs, I drove to John Skye's farm with Quinn beside me and my old .38 under the seat, a cold comfort at best.

"You're not going to leave me here," Quinn had said. "If you don't take me with you, I'll call a taxi."

So we went together and drove into John's yard with me not knowing what I'd find.

We found an empty yard, an empty barn, and an empty house in need of cleaning. Grace had never struck me as the housekeeper type, and Tom Rimini, Graham, and the others who'd been there clearly were not. Everything belonging to them was gone, but there was litter scattered in every room: overflowing ashtrays, pizza cartons, empty beer cans, crumpled newspapers, and other clutter. The lights were all on, and every bed was unmade, with sheets and blankets awry. Dirty glasses, plates, and silverware were everywhere except in the dishwasher. Someone had even started to read a book in John's library and had left it on the side table beside his favorite chair. I put the book back on its shelf and kicked at a wrinkled rug.

"Look on the bright side," said Quinn. "There's no blood anywhere and not a body in sight. You can have this place shipshape in half a day."

"While you and Zee are off fishing, of course."

"Of course. I'm a reporter for a great metropolitan newspaper. I don't clean houses."

We walked around the corrals and through the sheds and then through the barn again. The loft door was shut tight and the pad that had been on the floor was gone. There was no evidence of the rifleman who had lain in wait there yesterday.

"I have to clean this place up," I said when we got back to the house. "You take the truck. There's a fifty-fifty chance that these characters are in the standby line in Vineyard Haven, trying to get off. There's even a chance that Sonny and his crew are there, too, although I'm willing to bet that he was smart enough to get reservations off island either late last night or early this morning. You might try to get a photo or even an interview or two." His newsman's eyes brightened and I gave him a description of the four cars involved. I tossed him the keys and he headed for the Land Cruiser.

I went inside and phoned Zee and told her what I'd found and what I'd be doing for a few hours.

"So it's over," she said.

"This part of it, at least."

"I'll pick you up at noon."

I loaded up the dishwasher and the washing machine and got to work with a scrub brush, sponge, mop, and, finally, a vacuum cleaner. By the time Zee came by, the clotheslines were hung with sheets, pillowcases, and other once-soiled linens, the last of the dishes and silverware were back where they belonged, and there was no sign that the house had recently housed a pack of assassins.

As we drove home, the kids were in the rear compartment of Zee's little Jeep, goofing around and laughing about something. It was a good time to talk with their mother and not really be heard.

"I don't think I'll give John and Mattie all the details of Rimini's stay here," I said. "It might make them nervous, and I don't want that. People come to Martha's Vineyard to relax, not to fret about killers in their houses."

"The killers are gone," said Zee.

"But my guilty feelings aren't. I hate it

when I do stupid things, and one of my stupidest was misreading Tom Rimini. I thought I was doing a favor for a pretty normal guy with a gambling habit, but what I was really doing was helping a would-be gangster and his killer girlfriend set up an assassination attempt."

"How could you know? I think the assassination idea only came to him after you put him in John's house. I think he and that woman saw their chance to set a trap and decided to take it, knowing that Whelen was rash enough to walk into it. Everything just happened to fall into place. You couldn't have known because they didn't know, either, until after you'd hidden him there."

"I agree, but I still hate having been dumb enough to have set it up."

She glanced at me with those dark, dark eyes. "I don't think it was stupidity," she said. "I think it was love."

I felt a tighter breathing, and zero at the bone. "It's you I love," I said, but my voice sounded like stone.

She cocked her head to one side. "I know. But you still love her, too. Maybe not the way you love me, but it's still love. I don't think I feel quite the same way about Paul, but I'm still concerned about him. I want good things to happen to him. I know you want them to happen to Carla."

Zee had no evil in her. I was different. "Your ex is a jerk. He left you for another woman. You owe him nothing."

"And Carla left you for another man, and she was a fool, and you owe her nothing. But you still care for her, and that's why you tried to save Tom: so she'd have a chance to be happy. You're a good man, although you probably doubt it. It's one of the reasons I love you."

I stared out the windshield, then looked at her. Her face was almost free of the bruises Logan had inflicted, and her split lip was nearly healed, although I thought its scar would never quite leave. She was Woman, wiser than I in many ways, as strong or stronger than I was, more loving than I could be. I was astonished that of all the men in all the world she had chosen me.

"When Quinn gets back, we should go fishing," I said. "The tide will be right about two, and they're getting a lot of blues at Wasque and along East Beach."

"Sounds like a good plan," said Zee. I put a hand on her thigh and she gave me a cosmic smile.

Quinn never caught up with Rimini or McBride in Vineyard Haven, but he spoke to Dom Agganis, the Chief, and other island cops, and his nonstory of the mobsters' gatherings on the Vineyard made the front page of *The Globe*, and sparked exactly the kind of speculation he'd hoped for: What were they doing there? Why had they apparently abandoned their plans? Because they found themselves under surveillance by the sharp eyes of Vineyard police from the time they reached the island, or for some other mysterious reason?

The Gangsters in Paradise tale even made it to the national TV news, as did his interview, complete with photos, with Mrs. Zeolinda Jackson, wife, mother, nurse, and crack pistol shot. The latter was the ideal story, satisfying both the political left and right. The NRA headlined the pistol-owner-housewife-defends-house-and-home theme, and the radical women's groups rejoiced in the power of women to fend for themselves without depending on men to protect them. The fact that Zee was beautiful, as Quinn's photos revealed, and that she was totally uninterested in publicity, made it even better.

"You're a heroine," I said, turning off the TV at the end of the newscast. "Does that make me a hero?"

"You've always been a hero to me, sweets."

Tear-stained Diana came in. "Pa, Ma, I

can't find Mulder! Joshua says maybe Oliver Underfoot or Velcro ate him!"

Mulder was her goldfish. We went outside, and studied the fishpond.

"There he is," said Zee, pointing, as Mulder swam out from under a rock and joined Scully and the fellow fish. "Oliver Underfoot and Velcro wouldn't eat Mulder."

Atop the mound of dirt behind the fishpond and above the little waterfall that tumbled down into the pool was the white Greek temple we'd fashioned from scraps in the woodpile, and though most people would probably have found it pretty crude, it was our temple and we liked it. The fishpond and waterfall weren't bad either, for that matter. Maybe I had a future as a landscaper. If you planned to live on Martha's Vineyard, you couldn't have too many moneymaking skills, especially if, like me, you didn't want a regular job.

About a week later I got a call from Norman Aylward. "I've got some good news," he said. "Tomorrow the D.A. will call a press conference and announce that no charges will be brought against Mrs. Jackson. The killing of Pat Logan and the shooting of Howard Trucker were justifiable self-defense. I think his decision is legally correct and it is certainly politically correct."

"Thanks for the bulletin. Now maybe we can put this all behind us."

"Not quite. Sometime in the future they'll be putting Howie Trucker on trial for assault with a deadly weapon and whatever else the D.A. thinks they can stick him with. Zee will have to testify unless he pleads guilty or makes a plea bargain of some kind."

"I don't think Sonny Whelen would like to have Howie talking about family business, and I don't think Howie wants Sonny mad at him, so I doubt if there'll be any plea bargain, or at least not one involving ratting on Sonny."

"You may be right. We'll see. The important thing is that your wife is free and clear."

I wondered what the D.A. would have decided if the political winds had blown in a different direction, if, somehow, Zee had been portrayed in the press as less than a heroine. I wondered, too, how Logan's and Trucker's wives felt. Were they bitter? Angry? Relieved? I wondered what would become of them and their children. I wondered what Trucker, once a strong-arm man but now a guy with one bad arm and one bad leg, would do when he got out of jail.

Roads diverge in a yellow wood. Acts always have consequences that can't be anticipated.

I kept my eyes and ears open for news of Sonny Whelen and Pete McBride and any of the other actors in the little Vineyard melodrama in which I'd played a part, but it wasn't until late August that a small story appeared in *The Globe*: two bodies had been found in a car in Lynn. The police suspected foul play, which was not unknown in Lynn. I tried to remember the old verse:

Lynn, Lynn, city of sin;
You won't come out the way you went in.

By the next day, the story had gotten bigger. The dead men had been identified as Peter McBride and Albert "Bruno" Viti, both of whom were, as they say, "known to the police." A spokesman for the Lynn PD surmised that the killings were a manifestation of internecine conflict within the criminal community.

I thought the spokesman was right and was impressed by his language. When I'd been a Boston policeman, I'd never known anybody who used words like "manifestation of internecine conflict." Lynn was apparently getting a better-educated variety of cop these days.

I called Quinn and asked him if he'd heard anything about Graham. He said he'd heard that Graham had left town.

I called Carla, but her phone had been disconnected.

Hmmmmm.

About the same time, I bumped into Manny Fonseca down at the Dock Street Coffee Shop.

"Say," said Manny, "how's Zee doing?"

"Just fine. Getting her gear ready for the fishing derby."

"You think she might be willing to go back to shooting? There's a competition coming up that I'd like her to enter."

"I don't know, Manny. I haven't talked with her about it. Right after that business happened, though, she wanted no more to do with guns."

Manny nodded. "Yeah. I know how she felt. But maybe she's changed her mind."

"You can ask her."

"She's got the touch. It's a waste of talent if she gives up competition. She could be better than me, even."

High praise. "Ask her," I said. "She'll either say yes or no."

"Yeah, that's right. Okay, J.W., if it's okay with you, I'll do it. I'll ask her."

I didn't try to tell him that it didn't matter whether or not it was okay with me, because I wasn't Zee's manager or boss but only her husband. Instead, I said, "Do it, and good luck."

He came by the next evening and the two of them went up onto the balcony to talk while I got supper going. After a while, Manny came down alone.

"Zee says to go up and join her for a drink. I gotta go home. See ya." He waved a hand and went out. He looked happy.

I poured icy Luksusowa into a glass, added two green olives, and went up and sat beside Zee.

"I'm going to do it," she said. "I'm going to start practicing again. I thought for a while that I'd never touch a gun again, that there was something evil about me knowing enough about shooting to have done what I did to Logan and Trucker. But lately I've realized that what really bothered me was the idea that I could kill someone. I didn't want that to be true, and I was going to prove it wasn't by never shooting again. But now I've accepted it; I've accepted that part of me is willing to kill to defend myself and my family." She looked toward me. "I was afraid that you couldn't love me if I could do that."

I tried to choose the right words. "You

never have to be afraid of that. I love you because you can do it if you have to, but you'll
never do it if you don't have to." I said, "I
don't want an angel for a wife; I want a
woman who can be as strong as she has to
be. And that's what I have. Of course, if
you'd rather be considered a goddess . . ."

We stared out over the darkening waters.
Then she took my hand in hers. "If I decide
to be a goddess, does that mean I have to
start thinking of you as a god? I hope not,
because that would be very hard."

"I hate a vain deity," I said. "No, I'm content to be a mere mortal basking in your ce-
lestial radiance."

"Stop basking and slide that chair over
here," she said.

I did that. Her lips tasted like ambrosia.

That fall I got an envelope postmarked
from a town in Oklahoma. There was no return address. The envelope contained a
cashier's check for the amount I'd spent on
cell phones and the cash I'd given to Carla.
There was a brief note from her. Thanks for
everything. The Riminis were both
teaching, and the boys were in school.
Things were going well.

I hoped that they really were.

THREE RECIPES

QUICK COQ AU VIN

This is an excellent dish that is fast and easy to prepare.

> *Up to 8 pieces of chicken. (J. W. prefers dark meat, but Zee prefers white, so they usually use both.)*
> *1 ½ cups dry red wine*
> *1 package (1 ³/₈ oz.) onion soup mix*
> *1 beef bouillon cube*

Place all the ingredients in a 2-quart casserole, cover, and bake 2 hours at 350°.
Serve over rice or riced potatoes.

Serves 4 or more

GRILLED VEGETABLES

Even people who don't like vegetables like them when they're cooked like this.

Chop or slice your favorite vegetables into

bite-size pieces. J. W. and Zee usually use:
Onions
Red and/or green peppers
Summer squash and/or zucchini and what-
ever odds and ends of veggies they find in
the fridge
Portobello mushrooms
Eggplant

Parboil such veggies as carrots and broccoli.

Marinate the vegetables for a half hour, adding mushrooms and eggplant during last few minutes. J.W. and Zee use a combination of Good Seasons Garlic and Herb salad dressing, balsamic vinegar, and olive oil.

Place the vegetables in a grilling wok and grill over medium-high heat for 10 minutes, turning regularly.

Delish!

CLAM CHOWDER

There are as many chowders as there are chowder makers, and a lot of cooks never make it the same way twice. This is a good one, but feel free to alter it to suit your tastes.

J.W. digs his own clams, but you may want to buy yours at the grocery store.

1 large onion, chopped
4 or 5 slices of bacon cut into small pieces, or
    a small chunk of salt pork, cubed
2 cups diced potatoes
2 cups water
24 or more clams
¼ pound ground kielbasa
Salt and pepper
Hot pepper sauce
1 quart milk

Fry the onion and bacon (or salt pork) until the onion is pale and cooked.

Add potatoes and water and boil until the potatoes are done.

Meanwhile, steam the clams, and save the broth. Remove the meat from the shells and grind or chop it, then return it to the broth (using as much broth as suits your fancy) and add the potatoes, onion, kielbasa, and bacon (or salt pork), salt and pepper to taste, and a few shakes of hot pepper sauce.

At this point you can add the milk or you can freeze the chowder base for future use and add the milk later, after you've thawed and reheated the base.

The employees of Thorndike Press hope you have enjoyed this Large Print book. All our Large Print titles are designed for easy reading, and all our books are made to last. Other Thorndike Press Large Print books are available at your library, through selected bookstores, or directly from us.

For information about titles, please call:

(800) 223-1244
(800) 223-6121

To share your comments, please write:

Publisher
Thorndike Press
295 Kennedy Memorial Drive
Waterville, ME 04901